The Art of the Story-Teller

The Art of the Story-Teller

BY MARIE L. SHEDLOCK

FOREWORD BY ANNE CARROLL MOORE

THIRD EDITION, REVISED

WITH A NEW BIBLIOGRAPHY BY EULALIE STEINMETZ

SUPERVISOR OF STORYTELLING, THE NEW YORK PUBLIC LIBRARY

Dover Publications, Inc.

Published in Canada by General Publishing Company, Ltd., 30 Lesmill Road, Don Mills, Toronto, Ontario.
Published in the United Kingdom by Constable and Company, Ltd., 10 Orange Street, London WC 2.

This Dover edition, first published in 1951, is a reprint of the work originally published by D. Appleton & Company in 1915. This edition contains a new Foreword by Anne Carroll Moore and a revised List of Stories compiled by Eulalie Steinmetz.

International Standard Book Number: 0-486-20635-1

Library of Congress Catalog Card Number: 52-9976

Manufactured in the United States of America
Dover Publications, Inc.
180 Varick Street
New York, N. Y. 10014

FOREWORD

Marie L. Shedlock was born at Boulogne on May 5, 1854. She died in London in January, 1935.

No one who heard Marie Shedlock tell a story in English or in French will ever forget the music in her voice, the quality of her diction, her inimitable gesture, the sheer magic of her presentation of a complete drama in miniature.

"Personally I recall Miss Shedlock's story-telling, as I recall Patti's singing, Edwin Booth's acting, and Paderewski's playing, but there is nothing with which I can compare my recollections of Marie Shedlock's winsome personality and glowing friendliness," said Emma L. Johnston, for many years the Principal of Maxwell Training School for Teachers, in her tribute to the Story-telling Number of *The Horn Book,* published in May, 1934, in honor of Marie Shedlock's eightieth birthday. Fairy Godmother's Day it is called by the children, for to children of the United States and Canada she was and will continue to be a veritable fairy godmother whose gift to their countries is the story hour they know and love.

"I feel as much for one nation as for another," wrote Marie Shedlock from London when war began in 1914. "I have finished my book, putting into it all that seemed worth saving out of my lectures to teachers in America and England. Will it find an American publisher?" Her question was answered, when she came to New York the following year, by the late William W. Appleton who read the manuscript himself and enjoyed its humor and direct statement. Mr. Appleton, it may be recalled, was the publisher who first gave Alice in Wonderland an American setting. He was keenly interested in story-telling as a potent influence in stimulating the love of reading. As a trustee of The New York Public Library he was a frequent and always a welcome visitor to the story hours held in the branch libraries.

Miss Shedlock came for a six months visit in 1915 in response to the urgent invitation of fifty story-tellers she had herself brought into the field, reinforced by committees of representative women of New York and Boston. She remained in the United States and Canada for five years and had the pleasure and satisfaction of seeing the fruits of her earlier visits.

She would rejoice in the assurance that *The Art of the Story-Teller,* thirty-six years after its first publication, is regarded as the best, as it is the most readable, book on the subject.

Years of change, of progress, of sheer bewilderment in the educational world have not shaken Miss Shedlock's declaration of faith in the story as the natural introduction to literature, nor has the march of time obscured the wisdom embodied in her clear observations, sound suggestions, and intuitive understanding of children and childhood.

As a lifelong student of the literature of the Eastern as well as the Western World, Miss Shedlock was constantly adding to a repertoire of stories of extraordinary range and variety. She had a positive genius for building a program for an audience of children or of adults, and up to the last year of her life was warmly receptive to a new discovery among stories or a fresh translation of the tales of her own great master, Hans Christian Andersen—always provided no violence was done to the integrity of the tales she interpreted with such rare penetration and skill.

"I believe your work will last. What more can one artist say to another?" Marie Shedlock wrote in the copy of *The Art of the Story-Teller,* the first American edition of 1915, which she gave to Anna Cogswell Tyler in recognition of Miss Tyler's work as the organizer and Supervisor of Storytelling in The New York Public Library from 1908 until her death in 1923.

Anna Cogswell Tyler was succeeded by Mary Gould Davis who had been a student and associate of Miss Tyler for a number of years. Since her retirement from The New York Public Library in 1945 Miss Davis has continued the teaching and practice of story-telling over the country.

In offering a complete revision of the third section of the book its publishers are reinforcing in terms of contemporary interest a text which called for no alteration and have asked Eulalie Steinmetz, who succeeded Miss Davis as Supervisor of Storytelling in The New York Public Library, to bring the fruits of her own experience and judgment in carrying on a well-established tradition.

In Miss Tyler's memory I give back Marie Shedlock's words of 1915 to a third edition of a book in whose launching she and I shared editorial responsibility. For its saving common sense, its wit and wisdom Miss Tyler was, and I continue to be, eternally grateful on behalf of the storytelling of the future.

ANNE CARROLL MOORE

New York 1951

PREFACE TO THE ORIGINAL EDITION

Some day we shall have a science of education comparable to the science of medicine; but even when that day arrives the *art* of education will still remain the inspiration and the guide of all wise teachers. The laws that regulate our physical and mental development will be reduced to order; but the impulses which lead each new generation to play its way into possession of all that is best in life will still have to be interpreted for us by the artists who, with the wisdom of years, have not lost the direct vision of children.

Some years ago I heard Miss Shedlock tell stories in England. Her fine sense of literary and dramatic values, her power in sympathetic interpretation, always restrained within the limits of the art she was using, and her understanding of educational values, based on a wide experience of teaching, all marked her as an artist in story-telling. She was equally at home in interpreting the subtle blending of wit and wisdom in Daudet, the folk lore philosophy of Grimm, or the deeper world philosophy and poignant human appeal of Hans Christian Andersen.

Then she came to America and for two or three years she taught us the difference between the nightingale that sings in the tree tops and the artificial bird that goes with a spring. Cities like New York, Boston, Pittsburgh and Chicago listened and heard, if sometimes indistinctly, the notes of universal appeal, and children saw the Arabian Nights come true.

Yielding to the appeals of her friends in America and England, Miss Shedlock has put together in this little book such observations and suggestions on story-telling as can be put in words. Those who have the artist's spirit will find their sense of values quickened by her words, and they will be led to escape some of the errors into which even the greatest artists fall. And even those who tell stories with their minds will find in these papers wise generalizations and suggestions born of wide experience and extended study which will go far towards making even an artificial nightingale's song less mechanical. To those who know, the book is a revelation of the intimate relation between a child's instincts and the finished art of dramatic presentation. To those who do not know it will bring echoes of reality.

EARL BARNES

Philadelphia, 1915

CONTENTS

PART I

THE ART OF STORY-TELLING

PART II

THE STORIES

CONTENTS

PART III

A NEW LIST OF STORIES

CONTENTS

INTRODUCTION

Story-telling is almost the oldest art in the world—the first conscious form of literary communication In the East it still survives, and it is not an uncommon thing to see a crowd at a street corner held by the simple narration of a story. There are signs in the West of a growing interest in this ancient art, and we may yet live to see the renaissance of the troubadours and the minstrels whose appeal will then rival that of the mob orator or itinerant politician. One of the surest signs of a belief in the educational power of the story is its introduction into the curriculum of the training-college and the classes of the elementary and secondary schools. It is just at the time when the imagination is most keen, the mind being unhampered by accumulation of facts, that stories appeal most vividly and are retained for all time.

It is to be hoped that some day stories will be told to school groups only by experts who have devoted special time and preparation to the art of telling them. It is a great fallacy to suppose that the systematic study of story-telling destroys the spontaneity of narrative. After a long experience, I find the exact converse to be true, namely, that it is only when one has overcome the mechanical difficulties that one can "let one's self go" in the dramatic interest of the story.

By the expert story-teller I do not mean the professional elocutionist. The name, wrongly enough, has become associated in the mind of the public with persons who beat their breast, tear their hair, and declaim blood-curdling episodes. A decade or more ago, the drawing-room reciter was of this type, and was rapidly becoming the bugbear of social gatherings. The difference between the stilted reciter and the simple story-teller is perhaps best illustrated by an episode in Hans Christian Andersen's immortal "Story of the Nightingale." The real Nightingale and the artificial Nightingale have been bidden by the Emperor to unite their forces and to sing a duet at a Court function. The duet turns out most disastrously, and while the artificial Nightingale is singing his one solo for the thirty-third time, the real Nightingale flies out of the window back to the green wood—a true artist, instinctively choosing his right atmosphere. But the bandmaster—symbol of the pompous pedagogue—in trying to soothe the outraged feelings of the courtiers, says, "Because, you see, Ladies and Gentlemen, and, above all, Your Imperial Majesty, with the real nightingale you never can tell what you will hear, but in the artificial nightingale everything is decided beforehand. So it is, and so it must remain. It cannot be otherwise."

And as in the case of the two nightingales, so it is with the stilted reciter and the simple narrator: one is busy displaying the machinery, showing "how the tunes go"; the other is anxious to conceal the art. Simplicity should be the keynote of story-telling, but (and here the comparison with the nightingale breaks down) it is a simplicity which comes after much training in self-control, and much hard work in overcoming the difficulties which beset the presentation.

I do not mean that there are not born story-tellers who *could* hold an audience without preparation, but they are so rare in number that we can afford to neglect them in our general consideration, for this work is dedicated to the average story-tellers anxious to make the best use of their dramatic ability, and it is to them that I present my plea for special study and preparation before telling a story to a group of children—that is, if they wish for the far-reaching effects I shall speak of later on. Only the preparation must be of a much less stereotyped nature than that by which the ordinary reciters are trained for their career.

Some years ago, when I was in America, I was asked to put into the form of lectures my views as to the educational value of telling stories. A sudden inspiration seized me. I began to cherish a dream of long hours to be spent in the British Museum, the Congressional Library in Washington and the Public Library in Boston—and this is the only portion of the dream which has been realized. I planned an elaborate scheme of research work which was to result in a magnificent (if musty) philological treatise. I thought of trying to discover by long and patient researches what species of lullaby were crooned by Egyptian mothers to their babes, and what were the elementary dramatic poems in vogue among Assyrian nursemaids which were the prototypes of "Little Jack Horner," "Dickory, Dickory

Dock" and other nursery classics. I intended to follow up the study of these ancient documents by making an appendix of modern variants, showing what progress we had made—if any—among modern nations.

But there came to me suddenly one day the remembrance of a scene from Racine's "Plaideurs," in which the counsel for the defence, eager to show how fundamental his knowledge, begins his speech: "Before the Creation of the World"—And the Judge (with a touch of weariness tempered by humor) suggests:

"Let us pass on to the Deluge."

And thus I, too, have "passed on to the Deluge." I have abandoned an account of the origin and past of stories which at best would only have displayed a little recently acquired book knowledge. When I thought of the number of scholars who could treat this part of the question infinitely better than myself, I realized how much wiser it would be—though the task is more humdrum—to deal with the present possibilities of story-telling for our generation of parents and teachers.

My objects in urging the use of stories in the education of children are at least fivefold:

First, to give them dramatic joy, for which they have a natural craving; to develop a sense of humor, which is really a sense of proportion; to correct certain tendencies by showing the consequences in the career of the hero in the story [Of this motive the children must be quite unconscious and there should be no didactic emphasis]; to present by means of example, not precept, such ideals as will sooner or later be translated into action; and finally, to develop the imagination, which really includes all the other points.

But the art of story-telling appeals not only to the educational world and to parents as parents, but also to a wider public interested in the subject from a purely human point of view.

In contrast to the lofty scheme I had originally proposed to myself, I now simply place before all those who are interested in the art of story-telling in any form the practical experiences I have had in my travels in America and England.

I hope that my readers may profit by my errors, improve on my methods, and thus help to bring about the revival of an almost lost art.

In Sir Philip Sydney's "Defence of Poesie" we find these words:

"Forsooth he cometh to you with a tale, which holdeth children from play, and old men from the chimney-corner, and pretending no more, doth intend the winning of the mind from wickedness to virtue even as the child is often brought to take most wholesome things by hiding them in such other as have a pleasant taste."

MARIE L. SHEDLOCK

London, 1915

PART I

THE ART OF THE STORY-TELLER

CHAPTER I

THE DIFFICULTIES OF THE STORY

I propose to deal in this chapter with the difficulties or dangers which beset the path of the story-teller, because, until we have overcome these, we cannot hope for the finished and artistic presentation which is to bring out the full value of the story.

The difficulties are many, and yet they ought not to discourage the would-be narrators, but only show them how all-important is the preparation for the story, if it is to have the desired effect.

I propose to illustrate by concrete examples, thereby serving a twofold purpose: one to fix the subject more clearly in the mind of the student, the other to use the art of story-telling to explain itself.

I have chosen one or two instances from my own personal experience. The grave mistakes made in my own case may serve as a warning to others who will find, however, that experience is the best teacher. For positive work, in the long run, we generally find out our own method. On the negative side, however, it is useful to have certain pitfalls pointed out to us, in order that we may save time by avoiding them. It is for this reason that I sound a note of warning.

1. There is *the danger of side issues.* An inexperienced story-teller is exposed to the temptation of breaking off from the main dramatic interest in a short exciting story in order to introduce a side issue which is often interesting and helpful but which must be left for a longer and less dramatic story. If the interest turns on some dramatic moment, the action must be quick and uninterrupted, or it will lose half its effect.

I had been telling a class of young children the story of Polyphemus and Ulysses, and just at the most dramatic moment in the story some impulse for which I cannot account prompted me to go off on a side issue to describe the personal appearance of Ulysses.

The children were visibly bored, but with polite indifference they listened to my elaborate description of the hero. If I had given them an actual description from Homer, I believe that the strength of the language would have appealed to their imagination (all the more strongly because they might not have understood the individual words) and have lessened their disappointment at the dramatic issue being postponed; but I trusted to my own lame verbal efforts, and signally failed. Attention flagged, fidgeting began, the atmosphere was rapidly becoming spoiled in spite of the patience and toleration still shown by the children. At last, however, one little girl in the front row, as spokeswoman for the class, suddenly said: "If you please, before you go any further, do you mind telling us whether, after all, that Poly . . . [slight pause] . . . that . . . [final attempt] . . . *Polyanthus* died?"

Now, the remembrance of this question has been of extreme use to me in my career as a story-teller. I have realized that in a short dramatic story the mind of the listeners must be set at ease with regard to the ultimate fate of the special Polyanthus who takes the center of the stage.

I remember, too, the despair of a little boy at a dramatic representation of "Little Red Riding-Hood," when that little person delayed the thrilling catastrophe with the Wolf, by singing a pleasant song on her way through the wood. "Oh, why," said the little boy, "does she not get on?" And I quite shared his impatience.

This warning is necessary only in connection with the short dramatic narrative. There are occasions when we can well afford to offer short descriptions for the sake of literary style, and for the purpose of enlarging the vocabulary of the child. I have found, however, in these cases, it is well to take the children into your confidence, warning them that they are to expect nothing particularly exciting in the way of dramatic event. They will then settle down with a freer mind (though the mood may include a touch of resignation) to the description you are about to offer them.

2. *Altering the story to suit special occasions* is done sometimes from extreme conscientiousness, sometimes from sheer ignorance of the ways of children. It is the desire to protect them from knowledge which they already possess and with which they, equally conscientious, are apt to "turn and rend" the narrator. I remember once when I was telling the story of the Siege of Troy to very young children, I suddenly felt anxious lest there should be anything in the story of the rape of Helen not altogether suitable for the average age of the class, namely, nine years. I threw, therefore, a domestic coloring over the whole subject and presented an imaginary conversation between Paris and Helen, in which Paris tried to persuade Helen that she was a strong-minded woman thrown away on a limited society in Sparta, and that she should come away and visit some of the institutions of the world with him, which would doubtless prove a mutually instructive journey.[1] I then gave the children the view taken by Herodotus that Helen never went to Troy, but was detained in Egypt. The children were much thrilled by the story, and responded most eagerly when, in my inexperience, I invited them to repro-

[1] I venture to hope (at this long distance of years) that my language in telling the story was more simple than appears from this account.

duce in writing for the next day the story I had just told them.

A small child presented *me,* as you will see, with the ethical problem from which I had so laboriously protected *her.* The essay ran:

> Once upon a time the King of Troy's son was called Paris. And he went over to *Greace* to see what it was like. And here he saw the beautiful Helen*er,* and likewise her husband Menela*yus.* And one day, Menelayus went out hunting, and left Paris and Helener alone, and Paris said: "Do you not feel *dul* in this *palis?"*[1] And Helener said: "I feel very dull in this *pallice,"*[1] and Paris said: "Come away and see the world with me." So they *sliped* off together, and they came to the King of Egypt, and *he* said: "Who *is* the young lady"? So Paris told him. "But," said the King, "it is not *propper* for you to go off with other people's *wifes.* So Helener shall stop here." Paris stamped his foot. When Menelayus got home, *he* stamped his foot. And he called round him all his soldiers, and they stood round Troy for eleven years. At last they thought it was no use *standing* any longer, so they built a wooden horse in memory of Helener and the Trojans and it was taken into the town.

Now, the mistake I made in my presentation was to lay any particular stress on the reason for elopement by my careful readjustment, which really

[1] This difference of spelling in the same essay will be much appreciated by those who know how gladly children offer an orthographical alternative, in hopes that one if not the other may satisfy the exigency of the situation.

called more attention to the episode than was necessary for the age of my audience; and evidently caused confusion in the minds of some of the children who knew the story in its more accurate original form.

While traveling in America, I was provided with a delightful appendix to this story. I had been telling Miss Longfellow and her sister the little girl's version of the Siege of Troy, and Mrs. Thorpe made the following comment, with the American humor the dryness of which adds so much to its value:

"I never realized before," she said, "how glad the Greeks must have been to sit down even inside a horse, when they had been *standing* for eleven years."

3. *The danger of introducing unfamiliar words* is the very opposite danger of the one to which I have just alluded; it is the taking for granted that children are acquainted with the meaning of certain words upon which turns some important point in the story. We must not introduce, without at least a passing explanation, words which, if not rightly understood, would entirely alter the picture we wish to present.

I had once promised to tell stories to an audience of Irish peasants, and I should like to state here that, though my travels have brought me in touch with almost every kind of audience, I have never found one where the atmosphere is so "self-prepared" as in that of a group of Irish peasants. To speak to them, especially on the subject of fairy-tales, is like playing on a delicate harp: the response is so quick and the sympathy so keen. Of course, the subject of fairy-tales is one which is completely familiar to them and comes into their everyday life. They have a feeling of awe with regard to fairies, which is very deep in some parts of Ireland.

On this particular occasion I had been warned by an artist friend who had kindly promised to sing songs between the stories, that my audience would be of varying age and almost entirely illiterate. Many of the older men and women, who could neither read nor write, had never been beyond their native village. I was warned to be very simple in my language and to explain any difficult words which might occur in the particular Indian story I had chosen for that night, namely, "The Tiger, the Jackal and the Brahman." It happened that the older portion of the audience had scarcely ever seen even pictures of wild animals. I profited by the advice and offered a word of explanation with regard to the tiger and the jackal. I also explained the meaning of the word Brahman—at a proper distance, however, lest the audience should class him with wild animals. I then went on with my story, in the course of which I mentioned a buffalo. In spite of the warning I had received, I found it impossible not to believe that the name of this animal would be familiar to any audience. I, therefore, went on with the sentence containing this word, and ended it thus: "And then the Brahman went a little further and met an old buffalo turning a wheel."

The next day, while walking down the village street, I entered into conversation with a thirteen-year-old girl who had been in my audience the night before and who began at once to repeat in her own words the Indian story in question. When she came to the particular sentence I have just quoted, I was greatly startled to hear *her* version, which ran thus: "And the priest went on a little further, and he met another old gentleman pushing a wheelbarrow." I stopped her at once, and not being able to identify the sentence as part of the story I had told, I questioned her a little more closely. I found that the word, "buffalo," had evidently conveyed to her mind an old "buffer" whose name was "Lo," probably taken to be an Indian form of appellation, to be treated with tolerance though it might not be Irish in sound. Then, not knowing of any wheel more familiarly than that attached to a barrow, the young narrator completed the picture in her own mind—doubtless, a vivid one—but which, one must admit, had lost something of the Indian atmosphere which I had intended to gather about it.

4. *The danger of claiming coöperation of the class by means of questions* is more serious for the

teacher than the child, who rather enjoys the process and displays a fatal readiness to give any sort of answer if only he can play a part in the conversation. If we could in any way depend on the children giving the kind of answer we expect, all might go well and the danger would be lessened; but children have a perpetual way of frustrating our hopes in this direction, and of landing us in unexpected bypaths from which it is not always easy to return to the main road without a very violent reaction. As illustrative of this, I quote from "The Madness of Philip," by Josephine Daskam Bacon, a truly delightful essay on child psychology in the guise of the lightest of stories.

The scene takes place in a kindergarten, where a bold and fearless visitor has undertaken to tell a story on the spur of the moment to a group of restless children.

She opens thus:

"Yesterday, children, as I came out of my yard, what do you think I saw?"

The elaborately concealed surprise in store was so obvious that Marantha rose to the occasion and suggested, "an el'phunt."

"Why, no. Why should I see an elephant in my yard? It was not *nearly* so big as that—it was a little thing."

"A fish," ventured Eddy Brown, whose eye fell upon the aquarium in the corner. The raconteuse smiled patiently.

"Now, how could a fish, a live fish, get into my front yard?"

"A dead fish," says Eddy.

He had never been known to relinquish voluntarily an idea.

"No; it was a little kitten," said the story-teller decidedly. "A little white kitten. She was standing right near a big puddle of water. Now, what else do you think I saw?"

"Another kitten," suggests Marantha, conservatively.

"No; it was a big Newfoundland dog. He saw the little kitten near the water. Now, cats don't like water, do they? What do they like?"

"Mice," said Joseph Zukoffsky abruptly.

"Well, yes, they do; but there were no mice in my yard. I'm sure you know what I mean. If they don't like *water, what* do they like?"

"Milk," cried Sarah Fuller confidently.

"They like a dry place," said Mrs. R. B. Smith. "Now, what do you suppose the dog did?"

It may be that successive failures had disheartened the listeners. It may be that the very range of choice presented to them and the dog alike dazzled their imagination. At all events, they made no answer.

"Nobody knows what the dog did?" repeated the story-teller encouragingly. "What would you do if you saw a little kitten like that?"

And Philip remarked gloomily:

"I'd pull its tail."

"And what do the rest of you think? I hope you are not as cruel as that little boy."

A jealous desire to share Philip's success prompted the quick response:

"I'd pull it too."

Now, the reason of the total failure of this story was the inability to draw any real response from the children, partly because of the hopeless vagueness of the questions, partly because, there being no time for reflection, children say the first thing that comes into their heads without any reference to their real thoughts on the subject.

I cannot imagine anything less like the enlightened methods of the best kindergarten teaching. Had Mrs. R. B. Smith been a real, and not a fictional, person, it would certainly have been her last appearance as a raconteuse in this educational institution.

5. *The difficulty of gauging the effect of a story upon the audience* rises from lack of observation and experience; it is the want of these qualities which leads to the adoption of such a method as I have just presented. We learn in time that want of expression on the faces of the audience and want of any kind of external response do not always mean either lack of interest or attention. There is often real interest deep down, but no power, or perhaps no wish, to display that interest, which is deliberately concealed at times so as to protect oneself from questions which may be put.

6. *The danger of overillustration.* After long experience, and after considering the effect produced on children when pictures are shown to them during the narration, I have come to the conclusion that the appeal to the eye and the ear at the same

time is of doubtful value, and has, generally speaking, a distracting effect: the concentration on one channel of communication attracts and holds the attention more completely. I was confirmed in this theory when I addressed an audience of blind people[1] for the first time, and noticed how closely they attended, and how much easier it seemed to them because they were so completely "undistracted by the sights around them."

I have often suggested to young teachers two experiments in support of this theory. They are not practical experiments, nor could they be repeated often with the same audience, but they are intensely interesting, and they serve to show the *actual* effect of appealing to one sense at a time. The first of these experiments is to take a small group of children and suggest that they should close their eyes while you tell them a story. You will then notice how much more attention is given to the intonation and inflection of the voice. The reason is obvious. With nothing to distract the attention, it is concentrated on the only thing offered the listeners, that is, sound, to enable them to seize the dramatic interest of the story.

We find an example of the dramatic power of the voice in its appeal to the imagination in one of the tributes brought by an old pupil to Thomas Edward Brown, Master at Clifton College:

[1] At the Congressional Library in Washington.

"My earliest recollection is that his was the most vivid teaching I ever received; great width of view and poetical, almost passionate, power of presentment. We were reading Froude's History, and I shall never forget how it was Brown's words, Brown's voice, not the historian's, that made me feel the great democratic function which the monasteries performed in England; the view became alive in his mouth." And in another passage: "All set forth with such dramatic force and aided by such a splendid voice, left an indelible impression on my mind." [1]

A second experiment, and a much more subtle and difficult one, is to take the same group of children on another occasion, telling them a story in pantomime form, giving them first the briefest outline of the story. In this case it must be of the simplest construction, until the children are able, if you continue the experiment, to look for something more subtle.

I have never forgotten the marvelous performance of a play given in London many years ago entirely in pantomime form. The play was called "L'Enfant Prodigue," and was presented by a company of French artists. It would be almost impossible to exaggerate the strength of that "silent appeal" to the public. One was so unaccustomed to reading meaning and development of character into gesture and facial expression that it was really a

[1] Letters of T. E. Brown, page 55.

revelation to most of those present—certainly to all Anglo-Saxons.

I cannot touch on this subject without admitting the enormous dramatic value connected with the cinematograph. Though it can never take the place of an actual performance, whether in story form or on the stage, it has a real educational value in its possibilities of representation which it is difficult to overestimate, and I believe that its introduction into the school curriculum, under the strictest supervision, will be of extraordinary benefit. The movement, in its present chaotic condition, and in the hands of a commercial management, is more likely to stifle than to awaken or stimulate the imagination, but the educational world is fully alive to the danger, and I am convinced that in the future of the movement good will predominate.[1]

The real value of the cinematograph in connection with stories is that it provides the background that is wanting to the inner vision of the average child, and does not prevent its imagination from filling in the details later. For instance, it would be quite impossible for the average child to get an idea from mere word-painting of the atmosphere of the polar regions as represented lately on the film in connection with Captain Scott's expedition, but any stories told later on about these regions would have an infinitely greater interest.

[1] Great changes have taken place in line with this prophecy in the past twenty years.

There is, however, a real danger in using pictures to illustrate the story, especially if it be one which contains a direct appeal to the imagination of the child and one quite distinct from the stories which deal with facts, namely, that you force the whole audience of children to see the same picture, instead of giving each individual child the chance of making his own mental picture. That is of far greater joy, and of much greater educational value, since by this process the child coöperates with you instead of having all the work done for him.

Queyrat, in his work on "La Logique chez l'Enfant," quotes Madame Necker de Saussure: "To children and animals actual objects present themselves, not the terms of their manifestations. For them thinking is seeing over again, it is going through the sensations that the real object would have produced. Everything which goes on within them is in the form of pictures, or rather, inanimate scenes in which life is partially reproduced. . . . Since the child has, as yet, no capacity for abstraction, he finds a stimulating power in words and a suggestive inspiration which holds him enchanted. They awaken vividly colored images, pictures far more brilliant than would be called into being by the objects themselves."

Surely, if this be true, we are taking from children that rare power of mental visualization by offering to their outward vision an *actual* picture.

I was struck with the following note by a critic of the *Outlook*, referring to a Japanese play but which bears quite directly on the subject in hand.

"First, we should be inclined to put insistence upon appeal by *imagination*. Nothing is built up by lath and canvas; everything has to be created by the poet's speech."

He alludes to the decoration of one of the scenes which consists of three pines, showing what can be conjured up in the mind of the spectator.

> Ah, yes. Unfolding now before my eyes
> The views I know: the Forest, River, Sea
> And Mist—the scenes of Ono now expand.

I have often heard objections raised to this theory by teachers dealing with children whose knowledge of objects outside their own little limited circle is so scanty that words we use without a suspicion that they are unfamiliar are really foreign expressions to them. Such words as sea, woods, fields, mountains, would mean nothing to them, unless some explanation were offered. To these objections I have replied that where we are dealing with objects that can actually be seen with the bodily eyes, then it is quite legitimate to show pictures of those objects before you begin the story, so that the distraction between the actual and mental presentation may not cause confusion; but, as the foregoing example shows, we should endeavor to accustom the children to seeing much more than the mere objects themselves, and in dealing with abstract qualities we must rely solely on the power and choice of words and dramatic qualities of presentation, and we need not feel anxious if the response is not immediate, nor even if it is not quick and eager.[1]

7. *The danger of obscuring the point of the story with too many details* is not peculiar to teachers, nor is it shown only in the narrative form. I have often heard really brilliant after-dinner stories marred by this defect. One remembers the attempt made by Sancho Panza to tell a story to Don Quixote. I have always felt a keen sympathy with the latter in his impatience over the recital.

"In a village of Estramadura there was a shepherd—no, I mean a goatherd—which shepherd or goatherd as my story says, was called Lope Ruiz—and this Lope Ruiz was in love with a shepherdess called Torralva, who was daughter to a rich herdsman, and this rich herdsman——"

"If this be thy story, Sancho," said Don Quixote, "thou wilt not have done these two days. Tell it concisely, like a man of sense, or else say no more."

"I tell it in the manner they tell all stories in my country," answered Sancho, "and I cannot tell it otherwise, nor ought your Worship to require me to make new customs."

"Tell it as thou wilt, then," said Don Quixote, "since it is the will of fate that I should hear it, go on."

[1] In further illustration of this point see "When Burbage Played," Austen Dobson, and "In the Nursery," Hans Andersen.

Sancho continued:

"He looked about him until he espied a fisherman with a boat near him, but so small that it could only hold one person and one goat. The fisherman got into the boat and carried over one goat; he returned and carried another; he came back again and carried another. Pray, sir, keep an account of the goats which the fisherman is carrying over, for if you lose count of a single one, the story ends, and it will be impossible to tell a word more. . . . I go on, then. . . . He returned for another goat, and another, and another and another——"

"*Suppose* them all carried over," said Don Quixote, "or thou wilt not have finished carrying them this twelve months!"

"Tell me, how many have passed already?" said Sancho.

"How should I know?" answered Don Quixote.

"See there, now! Did I not tell thee to keep an exact account? There is an end of the story. I can go no further."

"How can this be?" said Don Quixote. "Is it so essential to the story to know the exact number of goats that passed over, that if one error be made the story can proceed no further?"

"Even so," said Sancho Panza.

8. *The danger of overexplanation* is fatal to the artistic success of any story, but it is even more serious in connection with stories told from an educational point of view, because it hampers the imagination of the listener, and since the development of that faculty is one of our chief aims in telling these stories, we must leave free play, we must not test the effect, as I have said before, by the

material method of asking questions. My own experience is that the fewer explanations you offer, provided you have been careful with the choice of your material and artistic in the presentation, the more the child will supplement by his own thinking power what is necessary for the understanding of the story.

Queyrat says: "A child has no need of seizing on the exact meaning of words; on the contrary, a certain lack of precision seems to stimulate his imagination only the more vigorously, since it gives him a broader liberty and firmer independence." [1]

9. *The danger of lowering the standard* of the story in order to appeal to the undeveloped taste of the child is a special one. I am alluding here only to the story which is presented from the educational point of view. There are moments of relaxation in a child's life, as in that of an adult, when a lighter taste can be gratified. I allude now to the standard of story for school purposes.

There is one development of story-telling which seems to have been very little considered, either in America or in our own country, namely, the telling of stories to *old* people, and that not only in institutions or in quiet country villages, but in the heart of the busy cities and in the homes of these old people. How often, when the young people are able to enjoy outside amusements, the old people, neces-

[1] "Les jeux des enfants," page 16.

sarily confined to the chimney-corner and many unable to read much for themselves, might return to the joy of their childhood by hearing some of the old stories told them in dramatic form. Here is a delightful occupation for those of the leisured class who have the gift, and a much more effective way of capturing attention than the more usual form of reading aloud.

Lady Gregory, in talking to the workhouse folk in Ireland, was moved by the strange contrast between the poverty of the tellers and the splendors of the tale. She says:

"The stories they love are of quite visionary things; of swans that turn into kings' daughters, and of castles with crowns over the doors, and of lovers' flights on the backs of eagles, and music-loving witches, and journeys to the other world, and sleeps that last for seven hundred years."

I fear it is only the Celtic imagination that will glory in such romantic material; but I am sure the men and women of the poorhouse are much more interested than we are apt to think in stories outside the small circle of their lives.

CHAPTER II

THE ESSENTIALS OF THE STORY

It would be a truism to suggest that dramatic instinct and dramatic power of expression are naturally the first essentials for success in the art of story-telling, and that, without these, no story-teller would go very far; but I maintain that, even with these gifts, no high standard of performance will be reached without certain other qualities, among the first of which I place *apparent* simplicity, which is really the *art* of *concealing* the art.

I am speaking here of the public story-teller, or of the teacher with a group of children, not the spontaneous (and most rare) power of telling stories at the fireside by some gifted village grandmother, such as Béranger gives us in his poem, "Souvenirs du Peuple":

> Mes enfants, dans ce village,
> Suivi de rois, il passa;
> Voilà bien longtemps de celà!
> Je venais d'entrer en ménage,
> À pied grimpant le coteau,
> Où pour voir je m'étais mise.

> Il avait petit chapeau et redingote grise.
> Il me dit: Bon jour, ma chère.
> Il vous a parlé, grand'mère?
> Il vous a parlé?

I am skeptical enough to think that it is not the spontaneity of the grandmother but the art of Béranger which enhances the effect of the story told in the poem.

This intimate form of narration, which is delightful in its special surroundings, would fail to *reach,* much less *hold,* a large audience, not because of its simplicity, but often because of the want of skill in arranging material and of the artistic sense of selection which brings the interest to a focus and arranges the side lights. In short, the simplicity we need for the ordinary purpose is that which comes from ease and produces a sense of being able to let ourselves go, because we have thought out our effects. It is when we translate our instinct into art that the story becomes finished and complete.

I find it necessary to emphasize this point because people are apt to confuse simplicity of delivery with carelessness of utterance, loose stringing of sentences of which the only connections seem to be the ever-recurring use of "and" and "so," and "er . . .", this latter inarticulate sound having done more to ruin a story and distract the audience than many more glaring errors of dramatic form.

Real simplicity holds the audience because the

lack of apparent effort in the artist has the most comforting effect upon the listener. It is like turning from the whirring machinery of process to the finished article, which bears no traces of the making except the harmony and beauty of the whole, which make one realize that the individual parts have received all proper attention. What really brings about this apparent simplicity which insures the success of the story? It has been admirably expressed in a passage from Henry James' lecture on Balzac:

"The fault in the artist which amounts most completely to a failure of dignity is the absence of *saturation with his idea.* When saturation fails, no other real presence avails, as when, on the other hand, it operates, no failure of method fatally interferes."

I now offer two illustrations of the effect of this saturation, one to show that the failure of method does not prevent successful effect, the other to show that when it is combined with the necessary secondary qualities the perfection of art is reached.

In illustration of the first point, I recall an experience in the north of England when the head mistress of an elementary school asked me to hear a young, inexperienced girl tell a story to a group of very small children.

When she began, I felt somewhat hopeless, because of the complete failure of method. She seemed to have all the faults most damaging to the success of a speaker. Her voice was harsh, her gestures awkward, her manner was restless and melodramatic; but, as she went on I soon began to discount all these faults and, in truth, I soon forgot about them, for so absorbed was she in her story, so saturated with her subject, that she quickly communicated her own interest to her audience, and the children were absolutely spellbound.

The other illustration is connected with a memorable peep behind the stage, when the late M. Coquelin had invited me to see him in the greenroom between the first and second acts of "L'Abbé Constantin," one of the plays given during his last season in London, the year before his death. The last time I had met M. Coquelin was at a dinner party, where I had been dazzled by the brilliant conversation of this great artist in the rôle of a man of the world. But on this occasion I met the simple, kindly priest, so absorbed in his rôle that he inspired me with the wish to offer a donation for his poor, and, on taking leave, to ask for his blessing for myself. While talking to him, I had felt puzzled. It was only when I had left him that I realized what had happened, namely, that he was too thoroughly saturated with his subject to be able to drop his rôle during the interval, in order to assume the more ordinary one of host and man of the world.

Now, it is this spirit I would wish to inculcate into the would-be story-tellers. If they would apply themselves in this manner to their work, it would bring about a revolution in the art of presentation, that is, in the art of teaching. The difficulty of the practical application of this theory is the constant plea, on the part of the teachers, that there is not the time to work for such a standard in an art which is so apparently simple that the work expended on it would never be appreciated.

My answer to this objection is that, though the counsel of perfection would be to devote a great deal of time to the story, so as to prepare the atmosphere quite as much as the mere action of the little drama (just as photographers use time exposure to obtain sky effects, as well as the more definite objects in the picture), yet it is not so much a question of time as concentration on the subject, which is one of the chief factors in the preparation of the story.

So many story-tellers are satisfied with cheap results, and most audiences are not critical enough to encourage a high standard.[1] The method of "showing the machinery" has more immediate results, and it is easy to become discouraged over the drudgery which is not necessary to secure the approbation of the largest number. But, since I am dealing with

[1] A noted Greek gymnast struck his pupil, though he was applauded by the whole assembly. "You did it clumsily, and not as you ought, for these people would never have praised you for anything really artistic."

the essentials of really good story-telling, I may be pardoned for suggesting the highest standard and the means for reaching it.

Therefore, I maintain that capacity for work, and even drudgery, is among the essentials of story-telling. Personally, I know of nothing more interesting than watching the story grow gradually from mere outline into a dramatic whole. It is the same pleasure, I imagine, which is felt over the gradual development of a beautiful design on a loom. I do not mean machine-made work, which has to be done under adverse conditions in a certain time and which is similar to thousands of other pieces of work; but that work upon which we can bestow unlimited time and concentrated thought.

The special joy in the slowly-prepared story comes in the exciting moment when the persons, or even the inanimate objects, become alive and move as of themselves. I remember spending two or three discouraging weeks with Andersen's story of the "Adventures of a Beetle." I passed through times of great depression, because all the little creatures, beetles, ear-wigs, frogs, etc., behaved in such a conventional, stilted way, instead of displaying the strong individuality which Andersen had bestowed upon them that I began to despair of presenting a live company at all.

But one day, the *Beetle,* so to speak, "took the stage," and at once there was life and animation among the minor characters. Then the main work was done, and there remained only the comparatively easy task of guiding the movement of the little drama, suggesting side issues and polishing the details, always keeping a careful eye on the Beetle, that he might "gang his ain gait" and preserve to the full his own individuality.

There is a tendency in preparing stories to begin with detail work, often a gesture or side issue which one has remembered from hearing a story told, but if this is done before the contemplative period, only scrappy, jerky and ineffective results are obtained, on which one cannot count for dramatic effects. This kind of preparation reminds one of a young peasant woman who was taken to see a performance of "Wilhelm Tell," and when questioned as to the plot could only sum it up by saying, "I know some fruit was shot at."[1]

I realize the extreme difficulty teachers have to devote the necessary time to perfecting the stories they tell in school, because this is only one of the subjects they have to teach in an already overcrowded curriculum. To them I would offer this practical advice: Do not be afraid to repeat your stories.[2] If you did not undertake more than seven

[1] For further details on the question of preparation of the story, see chapter on "Questions Asked by Teachers."

[2] Sully says that children love exact repetition because of the intense enjoyment bound up with the process of imaginative realization.

stories a year, chosen with infinite care, and if you repeated these stories six times during the year of forty-two weeks, you would be able to do artistic and, therefore, lasting work; you would give a very great deal of pleasure to the children who delight in hearing a story many times. You would also be able to avoid the direct moral application, for each time a child hears a story artistically told, a little more of the meaning underlying the simple story will come to him without any explanation on your part. The habit of doing one's best instead of one's second-best means, in the long run, that one has no interest except in the preparation of the best, and the stories, few in number, polished and finished in style, will have an effect of which one can scarcely overstate the importance.

In the story of the "Swineherd," Hans Andersen says:

"On the grave of the Prince's father there grew a rose-tree. It only bloomed once in five years, and only bore one rose. But what a rose! Its perfume was so exquisite that whoever smelt it forgot at once all his cares and sorrows."

Lafcadio Hearn says:

"Time weeds out the errors and stupidities of cheap success, and presents the Truth. It takes, like the aloe, a long time to flower, but the blossom is all the more precious when it appears."

CHAPTER III

THE ARTIFICES OF STORY-TELLING

By this term I do not mean anything against the gospel of simplicity which I am so constantly preaching, but, for want of a better term, I use the word "artifice" to express the mechanical devices by which we endeavor to attract and hold the attention of the audience. The art of telling stories is, in truth, much more difficult than acting a part on the stage: First, because the narrator is responsible for the whole drama and the whole atmosphere which surrounds it. He has to live the life of each character and understand the relation which each bears to the whole. Secondly, because the stage is a miniature one, gestures and movements must all be so adjusted as not to destroy the sense of proportion. I have often noticed that actors, accustomed to the more roomy public stage, are apt to be too broad in their gestures and movements when they tell a story. The special training for the story-teller should consist not only in the training of the voice and in choice of language, but above all in power of delicate suggestion, which cannot always be used on the stage because this is hampered by the presence of *actual things.* The story-teller has to present these things to the more delicate organism of the "inward eye."

So deeply convinced am I of the miniature character of the story-telling art that I believe one never gets a perfectly artistic presentation of this kind in a very large hall or before a very large audience.

I have made experiments along this line, having twice told a story to an audience in America[1] exceeding five thousand, but on both occasions, though the dramatic reaction upon oneself from the response of so large an audience was both gratifying and stimulating, I was forced to sacrifice the delicacy of the story and to take from its artistic value by the necessity of emphasis, in order to be heard by all present.

Emphasis is the bane of all story-telling, for it destroys the delicacy, and the whole performance suggests a struggle in conveying the message. The indecision of the victory leaves the audience restless and unsatisfied.

Then, again, as compared with acting on the stage, in telling a story one misses the help of effective entrances and exits, the footlights, the costume, the facial expression of your fellow-actor which interprets so much of what you yourself say without further elaboration on your part; for, in

[1] At the Summer School at Chautauqua, New York, and at Lincoln Park, Chicago.

the story, in case of a dialogue which necessitates great subtlety and quickness in facial expression and gesture, one has to be both speaker and listener.

Now, of what artifices can we make use to take the place of all the extraneous help offered to actors on the stage? First and foremost, as a means of suddenly pulling up the attention of the audience, is the judicious art of pausing. For those who have not actually had experience in the matter, this advice will seem trite and unnecessary, but those who have even a little experience will realize with me the extraordinary efficacy of this very simple means. It is really what Coquelin spoke of as a "high light," where the interest is focused, as it were, to a point.

I have tried this simple art of *pausing* with every kind of audience, and I have very rarely known it to fail. It is very difficult to offer a concrete example of this, unless one is giving a "live" representation, but I shall make an attempt, and at least I shall hope to make myself understood by those who have heard me tell stories.

In Hans Christian Andersen's "The Princess on the Pea," the King goes down to open the door himself. Now, one may make this point in two ways. One may either say: "And then the King went to the door, and at the door there stood a real Princess," or, "And then the King went to the door, and at the door there stood—(pause)—a real Princess."

It is difficult to exaggerate the difference of effect produced by so slight a pause.[1] With children it means an unconscious curiosity which expresses itself in a sudden muscular tension. There is just time during that instant's pause to *feel,* though not to *formulate,* the question: "What is standing at the door?" By this means, half your work of holding the attention is accomplished. It is not necessary for me to enter into the psychological reason of this, but I strongly recommend those who are interested in the question to read the chapter in Ribot's work on this subject, "Essai sur l'Imagination Créatrice," as well as Mr. Keatinge's work on "Suggestion."

I would advise all teachers to revise their stories with a view to introducing the judicious pause, and to vary its use according to the age, the number, and, above all, the mood of the audience. Experience alone can insure success in this matter. It has taken me many years to realize the importance of this artifice.

Among other means for holding the attention of the audience and helping to bring out the points of the story is the use of gesture. I consider, however, that it must be a sparing use, and not of a broad or definite character. We shall never improve on the advice given by Hamlet to the actors on this subject: "See that ye o'erstep not the modesty of Nature."

---

[1] There must be no more emphasis in the second manner than the first.

And yet, perhaps, it is not necessary to warn story-tellers against abuse of gesture. It is more helpful to encourage them in the use of it, especially in Anglo-Saxon countries, where we are fearful of expressing ourselves in this way, and when we do the gesture often lacks subtlety. The Anglo-Saxon, when he does move at all, moves in solid blocks—a whole arm, a whole leg, the whole body—but if one watches a Frenchman or an Italian in conversation, one suddenly realizes how varied and subtle are the things which can be suggested by the mere turn of the wrist or the movement of a finger. The power of the hand has been so wonderfully summed up in a passage from Quintillian that I am justified in offering it to all those who wish to realize what can be done by gesture:

"As to the hands, without the aid of which all delivery would be deficient and weak, it can scarcely be told of what a variety of motions they are susceptible, since they almost equal in expression the power of language itself. For other parts of the body assist the speaker, but these, I may almost say, speak themselves. With our hands we ask, promise, call persons to us and send them away, threaten, supplicate, intimate dislike or fear; with our hands we signify joy, grief, doubt, acknowledgment, penitence, and indicate measure, quantity, number and time. Have not our hands the power of inciting, of restraining, or beseeching, of testifying approbation? . . . So that amidst the great diversity of tongues pervading all nations and people, the language of the hands appears to be a language common to all men." [1]

One of the most effective of artifices in telling stories to young children is the use of mimicry—the imitation of animals' voices and sounds in general is of never-ending joy to the listeners. However, I should wish to introduce a note of grave warning in connection with this subject. This special artifice can only be used by such narrators as have special aptitude and gifts in this direction. There are many people with good imaginative power but who are wholly lacking in the power of mimicry, and their efforts in this direction, however painstaking, remain grotesque and therefore ineffective. When listening to such performances, of which children are strangely critical, one is reminded of the French story in which the amateur animal painter is showing her picture to an undiscriminating friend:

"Ah!" says the friend, "this is surely meant for a lion?"

"No," says the artist (?), with some slight show of temper, "it is my little lap-dog."

Another artifice which is particularly successful with very small children is to insure their attention by inviting their coöperation before one actually

[1] From "Education of an Orator," Book II, Chapter 3.

begins the story. The following has proved quite effective as a short introduction to my stories when I was addressing large audiences of children:

"Do you know that last night I had a very strange dream, which I am going to tell you before I begin the stories? I dreamed that I was walking along the streets of —— [here would follow the town in which I happened to be speaking], with a large bundle on my shoulders, and this bundle was full of stories which I had been collecting all over the world in different countries; and I was shouting at the top of my voice: 'Stories! Stories! Stories! Who will listen to my stories?' And the children came flocking round me in my dream, saying: 'Tell *us* your stories. *We* will listen to your stories.' So I pulled out a story from my big bundle and I began in a most excited way, 'Once upon a time there lived a King and a Queen who had no children, and they——' Here a little boy, *very* much like that little boy I see sitting in the front row, stopped me, saying: 'Oh, I know *that* old story: it's Sleeping Beauty.'

"So I pulled out a second story, and began: 'Once upon a time there was a little girl who was sent by her mother to visit her grandmother——' Then a little girl, *so* much like the one sitting at the end of the second row, said: 'Oh! everybody knows that story! It's——' "

Here I would make a judicious pause, and then

the children in the audience would shout in chorus, with joyful superiority: "Little Red Riding-Hood!" before I had time to explain that the children in my dream had done the same.

This method I repeated two or three times, being careful to choose very well-known stories. By this time the children were all encouraged and stimulated. I usually finished with congratulations on the number of stories they knew, expressing a hope that some of those I was going to tell that afternoon would be new to them. I have rarely found this plan fail to establish a friendly relation between oneself and the juvenile audience. It is often a matter of great difficulty, not to *win* the attention of an audience but to *keep* it, and one of the most subtle artifices is to let the audience down (without their perceiving it) after a dramatic situation, so that the reaction may prepare them for the interest of the next situation.

An excellent instance of this is to be found in Rudyard Kipling's story of "The Cat That Walked by Himself" where the repetition of words acts as a sort of sedative until one realizes the beginning of a fresh situation.

The great point is never to let the audience quite down, that is, in stories which depend on dramatic situations. It is just a question of shade and color in the language. If you are telling a story in sections, and one spread over two or three occasions, you should always stop at an exciting moment. It encourages speculation in the children's minds, which increases their interest when the story is taken up again.

Another very necessary quality in the mere artifice of story-telling is to watch your audience, so as to be able to know whether its mood is for action or reaction, and to alter your story accordingly. The moods of reaction are rarer, and you must use them for presenting a different kind of material. Here is your opportunity for introducing a piece of poetic description, given in beautiful language, to which the children cannot listen when they are eager for action and dramatic excitement.

Perhaps one of the greatest artifices is to take a quick hold of your audience by a striking beginning which will enlist their attention from the start. You can then relax somewhat, but you must be careful also of the end because that is what remains most vivid for the children. If you question them as to which story they like best in a program, you will constantly find it to be the last one you have told, which has for the moment blurred out the others.

Here are a few specimens of beginnings which seldom fail to arrest the attention of the child:

"There was once a giant ogre, and he lived in a cave by himself." From "The Giant and the Jackstraws": "The Book of Knight and Barbara," David Starr Jordan.

"There were once twenty-five tin soldiers, who were all brothers, for they had been made out of the same old tin spoon." From "The Tin Soldier," Hans Christian Andersen.

"There was once an Emperor who had a horse shod with gold." From "The Beetle," Hans Christian Andersen.

"There was once a merchant who was so rich that he could have paved the whole street with gold, and even then he would have had enough for a small alley." From "The Flying Trunk," Hans Christian Andersen.

"There was once a shilling which came forth from the mint springing and shouting, 'Hurrah! Now I am going out into the wide world.'" From "The Silver Shilling," Hans Christian Andersen.

"In the High and Far Off Times the Elephant, O Best Beloved, had no trunk." From "The Elephant's Child": "Just So Stories," Rudyard Kipling.

"Not always was the Kangaroo as now we behold him, but a Different Animal with four short legs." From "Old Man Kangaroo": "Just So Stories," Rudyard Kipling.

"Whichever way I turn," said the weather-cock on a high steeple, "no one is satisfied." From "Fireside Fables," Edwin Barrow.

"A set of chessmen, left standing on their board, resolved to alter the rules of the game." From the same source.

"The Pink Parasol had tender whalebone ribs and a slender stick of cherry-wood." From "Very Short Stories," Mrs. W. K. Clifford.

"There was once a poor little Donkey on Wheels: it had never wagged its tail, or tossed its head, or said 'Hee-haw,' or tasted a tender thistle." From the same source.

Now, some of these beginnings are, of course, for very young children, but they all have the same advantage, that of plunging *in medias res,* and, therefore, arrest attention at once, contrary to the stories which open on a leisurely note of description.

In the same way we must be careful about the endings of the stories. They must impress themselves either in a very dramatic climax to which the whole story has worked up, as in the following:

"Then he goes out to the Wet Wild Woods, or up the Wet Wild Trees, or on the Wet Wild Roofs, waving his Wild Tail, and walking by his Wild Lone." From "Just So Stories," Rudyard Kipling.

Or by an anti-climax for effect:

"We have all this straight out of the alderman's newspaper, but it is not to be depended on." From "Jack the Dullard," Hans Christian Andersen.

Or by evading the point:

"Whoever does not believe this must buy shares in the Tanner's yard." From "A Great Grief," Hans Christian Andersen.

Or by some striking general comment:

"He has never caught up with the three days he missed at the beginning of the world, and he has never learnt how to behave." From "How the Camel got his Hump": "Just So Stories," Rudyard Kipling.

I have only suggested in this chapter a few of the artifices which I have found useful in my own experience, but I am sure that many more might be added.

CHAPTER IV

ELEMENTS TO AVOID IN SELECTION OF MATERIAL

I am confronted in this portion of my work with a great difficulty, because I cannot afford to be as catholic as I could wish (this rejection or selection of material being primarily intended for those story-tellers dealing with normal children) ; but I do wish from the outset to distinguish between a story told to an individual child in the home circle or by a personal friend, and a story told to a group of children as part of the school curriculum. And if I seem to reiterate this difference, it is because I wish to show very clearly that the recital of parents and friends may be quite separate in content and manner from that offered by the teaching world. In the former case, almost any subject can be treated, because, knowing the individual temperament of the child, a wise parent or friend knows also what can be presented or not presented to the child; but in dealing with a group of normal children in school much has to be eliminated that could be given fearlessly to the abnormal child; I mean the child who, by circumstances or temperament, is developed beyond his years.

I shall now mention some of the elements which experience has shown me to be unsuitable for class stories.

1. *Stories dealing with analysis of motive and feeling.* This warning is specially necessary today, because this is, above all, an age of introspection and analysis. We have only to glance at the principal novels and plays during the last quarter of a century, more especially during the last ten years, to see how this spirit has crept into our literature and life.

Now, this tendency to analyze is obviously more dangerous for children than for adults, because, from lack of experience and knowledge of psychology, the child's analysis is incomplete. It cannot see all the causes of the action, nor can it make that philosophical allowance for mood which brings the adult to truer conclusions.

Therefore, we should discourage the child who shows a tendency to analyze too closely the motives of its action, and refrain from presenting to them in our stories any example which might encourage them to persist in this course.

I remember, on one occasion, when I went to say good night to a little girl of my acquaintance, I found her sitting up in bed, very wide-awake. Her eyes were shining, her cheeks were flushed, and when I asked her what had excited her so much, she said:

"I *know* I have done something wrong today, but I cannot quite remember what it was."

I said: "But, Phyllis, if you put your hand, which is really quite small, in front of your eyes, you could not see the shape of anything else, however large it might be. Now, what you have done today appears very large because it is so close, but when it is a little further off, you will be able to see better and know more about it. So let us wait till tomorrow morning."

I am happy to say that she took my advice. She was soon fast asleep, and the next morning she had forgotten the wrong over which she had been unhealthily brooding the night before.

2. *Stories dealing too much with sarcasm and satire.* These are weapons which are too sharply polished, and therefore too dangerous, to place in the hands of children. For here again, as in the case of analysis, they can only have a very incomplete conception of the case. They do not know the real cause which produces the apparently ridiculous situation. It is experience and knowledge which lead to the discovery of the pathos and sadness which often underlie the ridiculous appearance, and it is only the abnormally gifted child or grown-up person who discovers this by instinct. It takes a lifetime to arrive at the position described in Sterne's

words: "I would not have let fallen an unseasonable pleasantry in the venerable presence of misery to be entitled to all the wit which Rabelais has ever scattered."

I will hasten to add that I should not wish children to have their sympathy too much drawn out, or their emotions kindled too much to pity, because this would be neither healthy nor helpful to themselves or others. I only want to protect children from the dangerous critical attitude induced by the use of satire which sacrifices too much of the atmosphere of trust and belief in human beings which ought to be an essential of childlife. By indulging in satire, the sense of kindness in children would become perverted, their sympathy cramped, and they themselves would be old before their time. We have an excellent example of this in Hans Christian Andersen's "Snow Queen."

When Kay gets the piece of broken mirror into his eye, he no longer sees the world from the normal child's point of view; he can no longer see anything but the foibles of those about him, a condition usually reached only by a course of pessimistic experience.

Andersen sums up the unnatural point of view in these words: "When Kay tried to repeat the Lord's Prayer, he could only remember the multiplication-table." Now, without taking these words in any literal sense, we can admit that they represent the development of the head at the expense of the heart.

An example of this kind of story to avoid is Andersen's "Story of the Butterfly." The bitterness of the Anemones, the sentimentality of the Violets, the schoolgirlishness of the Snowdrops, the domesticity of the Sweetpeas—all this tickles the palate of the adult, but does not belong to the plane of the normal child. Again, I repeat, that the unusual child may take all this in and even preserve his kindly attitude towards the world, but it is dangerous atmosphere for the ordinary child.

3. *Stories of a sentimental character.* Strange to say, this element of sentimentality appeals more to the young teachers than to the children themselves. It is difficult to define the difference between real sentiment and sentimentality, but the healthy normal boy or girl of, let us say, ten or eleven years old, seems to feel it unconsciously, though the distinction is not so clear a few years later.

Mrs. Elisabeth McCracken contributed an excellent article some years ago to the *Outlook* on the subject of literature for the young, in which we find a good illustration of this power of discrimination on the part of a child.

A young teacher was telling her pupils the story of the emotional lady who, to put her lover to the test, bade him pick up the glove which she had thrown down into the arena between the tiger and the lion. The lover does her bidding in order to vindicate his character as a brave knight. One boy after hearing the story at once states his contempt for the knight's acquiescence, which he declares to be unworthy.

"But," says the teacher, "you see he really did it to show the lady how foolish she was." The answer of the boy sums up what I have been trying to show: "There was no sense in *his* being sillier than *she* was, to show her *she* was silly."

If the boy had stopped there, we might have concluded that he was lacking in imagination or romance, but his next remark proves what a balanced and discriminating person he was, for he added: "Now, if *she* had fallen in, and he had leapt after her to rescue her, that would have been splendid and of some use." Given the character of the lady, we might, as adults, question the last part of the boy's statement, but this is pure cynicism and fortunately does not enter into the child's calculations.

In my own personal experience, and I have told this story often in the German ballad form to girls of ten and twelve in the high schools in England, I have never found one girl who sympathized with the lady or who failed to appreciate the poetic justice meted out to her in the end by the dignified renunciation of the knight.

Chesterton defines sentimentality as "a tame, cold,

or small and inadequate manner of speaking about certain matters which demand very large and beautiful expression."

I would strongly urge upon young teachers to revise, by this definition, some of the stories they have included in their repertories, and see whether they would stand the test or not.

4. *Stories containing strong sensational episodes.* The danger of this kind of story is all the greater because many children delight in it and some crave for it in the abstract, but fear it in the concrete.[1]

An affectionate aunt, on one occasion, anxious to curry favor with a four-year-old nephew, was taxing her imagination to find a story suitable for his tender years. She was greatly startled when he suddenly said, in a most imperative tone: "Tell me the story of a bear eating a small boy." This was so remote from her own choice of subject that she hesitated at first, but coming to the conclusion that as the child had chosen the situation he would feel no terror in the working up of its details, she began a most thrilling and blood-curdling story, leading up to the final catastrophe. But just as she had reached the great dramatic moment, the child raised his hands in terror and said: "Oh! Auntie, don't let the bear *really* eat the boy!"

"Don't you know," said an impatient boy who had

[1] One child's favorite book bore the exciting title of "Birth, Life and Death of Crazy Jane."

been listening to a mild adventure story considered suitable to his years, "that I don't take any interest in the story until the decks are dripping with gore?" Here we have no opportunity of deciding whether or not the actual description demanded would be more alarming than the listener had realized.

Here is a poem of James Stephens, showing a child's taste for sensational things:

A man was sitting underneath a tree
Outside the village, and he asked me
What name was upon this place, and said he
Was never here before. He told a
Lot of stories to me too. His nose was flat.
I asked him how it happened, and he said,
The first mate of the *Mary Ann* done that
With a marling-spike one day, but he was dead,
And a jolly job too, but he'd have gone a long way to have killed him.
A gold ring in one ear, and the other was bit off by a crocodile, bedad,
That's what he said: He taught me how to chew.
He was a real nice man. He liked me too.

The taste that is fed by the sensational contents of the newspapers and the dramatic excitement of street life, and some of the lurid representations of the cinematograph, is so much stimulated that the interest in normal stories is difficult to rouse. I will not here dwell on the deleterious effects of over-dramatic stimulation, which has been known to lead to crime, since I am keener to prevent the telling of too many sensational stories than to suggest a cure when the mischief is done.

Kate Douglas Wiggin has said:

"Let us be realistic, by all means, but beware, O story-teller, of being too realistic. Avoid the shuddering tale of 'the wicked boy who stoned the birds,' lest some hearer should be inspired to try the dreadful experiment and see if it really does kill."

I must emphasize the fact, however, that it is only the excess of this dramatic element which I deplore. A certain amount of excitement is necessary, but this question belongs to the positive side of the subject, and I shall deal with it later on.

5. *Stories presenting matters quite outside the plane of a child's interests, unless they are wrapped in mystery.* Experience with children ought to teach us to avoid stories which contain too much *allusion* to matters of which the hearers are entirely ignorant. But, judging from the written stories of today, supposed to be for children, it is still a matter of difficulty to realize that this form of allusion to "foreign" matters, or making a joke, the appreciation of which depends solely on a special and "inside" knowledge, is always bewildering and fatal to sustained dramatic interest.

It is a matter of intense regret that so very few people have sufficiently clear remembrance of their own childhood to help them to understand the taste and point of view of the *normal* child. There is a passage in the "Brownies," by Mrs. Ewing, which illustrates the confusion created in the child mind by a facetious allusion in a dramatic moment which needed a more direct treatment. When the nursery toys have all gone astray, one little child exclaims joyfully:

"Why, the old Rocking Horse's nose has turned up in the oven!"

"It couldn't," remarks a tiresome, facetious doctor, far more anxious to be funny than to sympathize with the joy of the child, "it was the purest Grecian, modeled from the Elgin marbles."

Now, for grown-up people this is an excellent joke, but for a child who has not yet become acquainted with these Grecian masterpieces, the whole remark is pointless and hampering.[1]

6. *Stories which appeal to fear or priggishness.* This is a class of story which scarcely counts today and against which the teacher does not need a warning, but I wish to make a passing allusion to these stories, partly to round off my subject and partly to show that we have made some improvement in choice of subject.

When I study the evolution of the story from the crude recitals offered to our children within the last hundred years, I feel that, though our progress may

[1] This does not imply that the child would not appreciate in the right context the thrilling and romantic story in connection with the finding of the Elgin marbles.

be slow, it is real and sure. One has only to take some examples from the Chap Books of the beginning of last century to realize the difference of appeal. Everything offered then was either an appeal to fear or to priggishness, and one wonders how it is that our grandparents and their parents ever recovered from the effects of such stories as were offered to them. But there is the consoling thought that no lasting impression was made upon them, such as I believe *may* be possible by the right kind of story.

I offer a few examples of the old type of story:

Here is an encouraging address offered to children by a certain Mr. Janeway about the year 1828:

"Dare you do anything which your parents forbid you, and neglect to do what they command? Dare you to run up and down on the Lord's Day, or do you keep in to read your book, and learn what your good parents command?"

Such an address would have almost tempted children to envy the lot of orphans, except that the guardians and less close relations might have been equally, if not more, severe.

From "The Curious Girl," published about 1809:

"Oh! papa, I hope you will have no reason to be dissatisfied with me, for I love my studies very much, and I am never so happy at my play as when I have been assiduous at my lessons all day."

"Adolphus: How strange it is, papa, you should

believe it possible for me to act so like a child, now that I am twelve years old!"

Here is a specimen taken from a Chap Book about 1825:

Edward refuses hot bread at breakfast. His hostess asks whether he likes it.

"Yes, I am extremely fond of it."

"Why did you refuse it?"

"Because I know that my papa does not approve of my eating it. Am I to disobey a Father and Mother I love so well, and forget my duty, because they are a long way off? I would not touch the cake, were I sure nobody could see me. I myself should know it, and that would be sufficient."

"Nobly replied!" exclaimed Mrs. C. "Act always thus, and you must be happy, for although the whole world should refuse the praise that is due, you must enjoy the approbation of your conscience, which is beyond anything else."

Here is a quotation of the same kind from Mrs. Sherwood:

Tender-souled little creatures, desolated by a sense of sin, if they did but eat a spoonful of cupboard jam without Mamma's express permission. . . . Would a modern Lucy, jealous of her sister Emily's doll, break out thus easily into tearful apology for her guilt: 'I know it is wicked in me to be sorry that Emily is happy, but I feel that I cannot help it'? And would a modern mother retort with heartfelt joy: 'My dear child, I am glad you have confessed. Now I shall tell you why you feel this wicked sorrow'?—proceeding to an account of the depravity of human nature so unredeemed by comfort for a childish mind of common intelligence that one can scarcely imagine the interview ending in anything less tragic than a fit of juvenile hysteria.

Description of a good boy:

A good boy is dutiful to his Father and Mother, obedient to his master and loving to his playfellows. He is diligent in learning his book and takes a pleasure in improving himself in everything that is worthy of praise. He rises early in the morning, makes himself clean and decent, and says his prayers. He loves to hear good advice, is thankful to those who give it and always follows it. He never swears[1] or calls names or uses ill words to companions. He is never peevish and fretful, always cheerful and good-tempered.

7. *Stories of exaggerated and coarse fun.* In the chapter on the positive side of this subject I shall speak more in detail of the educational value of robust and virile representation of fun and of sheer nonsense, but as a preparation to these statements, I should like to strike a note of warning against the element of exaggerated and coarse fun being encouraged in our school stories, partly, because of the lack of humor in such presentations (a natural product of stifling imagination) and partly, because the strain of the abnormal has the same

[1] One is almost inclined to prefer Marjorie Fleming's little innocent oaths.

"But she was more than usual calm,
She did not give a single dam."

effect as the too frequent use of the melodramatic.

In an article in *Macmillan's Magazine,* December, 1869, Miss Yonge writes:

"A taste for buffoonery is much to be discouraged, an exclusive taste for extravagance most unwholesome and even perverting. It becomes destructive of reverence and soon degenerates into coarseness. It permits nothing poetical or imaginative, nothing sweet or pathetic to exist, and there is a certain self-satisfaction and superiority in making game of what others regard with enthusiasm and sentiment which absolutely bars the way against a higher or softer tone."

Although these words were written nearly half a century ago, they are so specially applicable today that they seem quite "up-to-date." Indeed, I think they will hold equally good fifty years hence.

In spite of a strong taste on the part of children for what is ugly and brutal, I am sure that we ought to eliminate this element as far as possible from the school stories, especially among poor children. Not because I think children should be protected from all knowledge of evil, but because so much of this knowledge comes into their life outside school that we can well afford to ignore it during school hours. At the same time, however, as I shall show by example when I come to the positive side, it would be well to show children by story illustration the difference between brutal ugliness without anything to redeem it and surface ugliness, which may be only a veil over the beauty that lies underneath. It might be possible, for instance, to show children the difference between the real ugliness of a brutal story of crime and an illustration of it in the sensational papers, and the apparent ugliness in the priest's face of the "Laocoon" group, because of the motive of courage and endurance behind the suffering. Many stories in everyday life could be found to illustrate this.

8. *Stories of infant piety and death-bed scenes.* The stories for children forty years ago contained much of this element, and the following examples will illustrate this point:

Notes from poems written by a child between six and eight years of age, by name Philip Freeman, afterwards Archdeacon of Exeter:

> Poor Robin, thou canst fly no more,
> Thy joys and sorrows all are o'er.
> Through Life's tempestuous storms thou'st trod,
> But now art sunk beneath the sod.
> Here lost and gone poor Robin lies,
> He trembles, lingers, falls and dies.
> He's gone, he's gone, forever lost,
> No more of him they now can boast.
> Poor Robin's dangers all are past,
> He struggled to the very last.
> Perhaps he spent a happy Life,
> Without much struggle and much strife.[1]

[1] Published by John Loder, bookseller, Woodbridge, in 1829.

The prolonged gloom of the main theme is somewhat lightened by the speculative optimism of the last verse.

> Life, transient Life, is but a dream,
> Like Sleep which short doth lengthened seem
> Till dawn of day, when the bird's lay
> Doth charm the soul's first peeping gleam
>
> Then farewell to the parting year,
> Another's come to Nature dear.
> In every place, thy brightening face
> Does welcome winter's snowy drear.
>
> Alas! our time is much mis-spent.
> Then we must haste and now repent.
> We have a book in which to look,
> For we on Wisdom should be bent.
>
> Should God, the Almighty, King of all,
> Before His judgment-seat now call
> Us to that place of Joy and Grace
> Prepared for us since Adam's fall.

I think there is no doubt that we have made considerable progress in this matter. Not only do we refrain from telling these highly moral (*sic*) stories but we have reached the point of parodying them, in sign of ridicule, as, for instance, in such writing as Belloc's "Cautionary Tales." These would be a trifle too grim for a timid child, but excellent fun for adults.

It should be our study today to prove to children that the immediate importance to them is not to think of dying and going to Heaven, but of living and—shall we say?—of going to college, which is a far better preparation for the life to come than the morbid dwelling upon the possibility of an early death.

In an article signed "Muriel Harris," I think, from a copy of the *Tribune,* appeared a delightful article on Sunday books, from which I quote the following:

"All very good little children died young in the story-books, so that unusual goodness must have been the source of considerable anxiety to affectionate parents. I came across a little old book the other day called 'Examples for Youth.' On the yellow fly-leaf was written, in childish, carefully-sloping hand: 'Presented to Mary Palmer Junior, by her sister, to be read on Sundays,' and was dated 1828. The accounts are taken from a work on 'Piety Promoted,' and all of them begin with unusual piety in early youth and end with the death-bed of the little paragon, and his or her dying words."

9. *Stories containing a mixture of fairy tale and science.* By this combination one loses what is essential to each, namely, the fantastic on the one side, and accuracy on the other. The true fairy tale should be unhampered by any compromise of probability even; the scientific representation should be

sufficiently marvelous along its own lines to need no supernatural aid. Both appeal to the imagination in different ways.

As an exception to this kind of mixture, I should quote "The Honey Bee, and Other Stories," translated from the Danish of Evald by C. G. Moore Smith. There is a certain robustness in these stories dealing with the inexorable laws of Nature. Some of them will appear hard to the child but they will be of interest to all teachers.

Perhaps the worst element in the choice of stories is that which insists upon the moral detaching itself and explaining the story. In "Alice in Wonderland" the Duchess says, " 'And the moral of *that* is: Take care of the sense and the sounds will take care of themselves.' 'How fond she is of finding morals in things,' thought Alice to herself." (This gives the point of view of the child.)

The following is a case in point, found in a rare old print in the British Museum:

Jane S. came home with her clothes soiled and hands badly torn. "Where have you been?" asked her mother.

"I fell down the bank near the mill," said Jane, "and I should have been drowned, if Mr. M. had not seen me and pulled me out."

"Why did you go so near the edge of the brink?"

"There was a pretty flower there that I wanted, and I only meant to take one step, but I slipped and fell down."

Moral: Young people often take but one step in sinful

indulgence [Poor Jane!], but they fall into soul-destroying sins. There is a sinful pleasure which they wish to enjoy. They can do it by a single act of sin. [The heinous act of picking a flower!] They do it; but that act leads to another, and they fall into the Gulf of Perdition, unless God interposes.

Now, quite apart from the folly of this story we must condemn it on moral grounds. Could we imagine a lower standard of a Deity than that presented here to the child?

Today the teacher would commend Jane for a laudable interest in botany, but might add a word of caution about choosing inclined planes in the close neighborhood of a body of running water as a hunting ground for specimens and a popular, lucid explanation of the inexorable law of gravity.

Here we have an instance of applying a moral when we have finished our story, but there are many stories where nothing is left to chance in this matter and where there is no means for the child to use ingenuity or imagination in making out the meaning for himself.

Henry Morley has condemned the use of this method as applied to fairy stories. He says: "Moralizing in a fairy story is like the snoring of *Bottom* in *Titania's* lap."

But I think this applies to all stories, and most especially to those by which we do wish to teach something.

John Burroughs says in his article, "Thou Shalt Not Preach": [1]

"Didactic fiction can never rank high. Thou shalt not preach or teach; thou shalt portray and create, and have ends as universal as nature. . . . What Art demands is that the artist's personal convictions and notions, his likes and dislikes, do not obtrude themselves at all; that good and evil stand judged in his work by the logic of events, as they do in nature, and not by any special pleading on his part. He does not hold a brief for either side; he exemplifies the working of the creative energy. . . . The great artist works *in* and *through* and *from* moral ideas; his works are indirectly a criticism of life. He is moral without having a moral. The moment a moral obtrudes itself, that moment he begins to fall from grace as an artist. . . . The great distinction of Art is that it aims to see life steadily and to see it whole. . . . It affords the one point of view whence the world appears harmonious and complete."

It would seem, then, from this passage, that it is of *moral* importance to put things dramatically.

In Froebel's "Mother Play" he demonstrates the educational value of stories, emphasizing that their highest use consists in their ability to enable the child, through *suggestion,* to form a pure and noble idea of what a man may be or do. The sensitive-

[1] From "Literary Values."

ness of a child's mind is offended if the moral is forced upon him, but if he absorbs it unconsciously, he has received its influence for all time.

To me the idea of pointing out the moral of the story has always seemed as futile as tying a flower on to a stalk instead of letting the flower grow out of the stalk, as Nature has intended. In the first case, the flower, showy and bright for the moment, soon fades away. In the second instance, it develops slowly, coming to perfection in fullness of time because of the life within.

Lastly, the element to avoid is that which rouses emotions which cannot be translated into action.

Mr. Earl Barnes, to whom all teachers owe a debt of gratitude for the inspiration of his educational views, insists strongly on this point. The sole effect of such stories is to produce a form of hysteria, fortunately short-lived, but a waste of force which might be directed into a better channel.[1] Such stories are so easy to recognize that it would be useless to make a formal list, but I make further allusion to them, in dealing with stories from the lives of the saints.

These, then, are the main elements to avoid in the selection of material suitable for normal children.

[1] A story is told of Confucius, who, having attended a funeral, presented his horse to the chief mourner. When asked why he bestowed this gift, he replied: "I wept with the man, so I felt I ought to *do* something for him."

Much might be added in the way of detail, and the special tendency of the day may make it necessary to avoid one class of story more than another, but this care belongs to another generation of teachers and parents.

CHAPTER V

ELEMENTS TO SEEK IN CHOICE OF MATERIAL

In his "Choice of Books," Frederic Harrison has said: "The most useful help to reading is to know what we shall *not* read, what we shall keep from that small, cleared spot in the overgrown jungle of information which we can call our ordered patch of fruit-bearing knowledge."

Now, the same statement applies to our stories, and, having busied myself during the last chapter with "clearing my small spot" by cutting away a mass of unfruitful growth, I am now going to suggest what would be the best kind of seed to sow in the patch which I have "reclaimed from the jungle."

Again, I repeat, I have no wish to be dogmatic and in offering suggestions as to the stories to be told, I am catering only for a group of normal school children. My list of subjects does not pretend to cover the whole ground of children's needs, and just as I exclude the abnormal or unusual child from the scope of my warning in subjects to avoid, so do I also exclude that child from the limitation in choice of subjects to be sought, because you can offer almost any subject to the unusual child, especially if you stand in close relation to him and know his powers of apprehension. In this matter, age has very little to say; it is a question of the stage of development.

Experience has taught me that for the group of normal children, irrespective of age, the first kind of story suitable for them will contain an appeal to conditions to which the child is accustomed. The reason for this is obvious: the child, having limited experience, can only be reached by this experience, until his imagination is awakened and he is enabled to grasp through this faculty what he has not actually passed through. Before this awakening has taken place he enters the realm of fiction, represented in the story, by comparison with his personal experience. Every story and every point in the story mean more as that experience widens, and the interest varies, of course, with temperament, quickness of perception, power of visualizing and of concentration.

In "The Marsh King's Daughter," Hans Christian Andersen says:

"The storks have a great many stories which they tell their little ones, all about the bogs and marshes. They suit them to their age and capacity. The young ones are quite satisfied with *kribble, krabble,* or some such nonsense, and find it charming; but the elder ones want something with more meaning."

One of the most interesting experiments to be made in connection with this subject is to tell the same story at intervals of a year or six months to an individual child.[1] The different incidents in the story which appeal to him (and one must watch it closely, to be sure the interest is real and not artificially stimulated by any suggestion on one's own part) will mark his mental development and the gradual awakening of his imagination. This experiment is a very delicate one and will not be infallible, because children are secretive and the appreciation is often simulated (unconsciously) or concealed through shyness or want of articulation. But it is, in spite of this, a deeply interesting and helpful experiment.

To take a concrete example: Let us suppose the story of Andersen's "Tin Soldier" told to a child of five or six years. At the first recital, the point which will interest the child most will be the setting up of the tin soldiers on the table, because he can understand this by means of his own experience, in his own nursery. It is an appeal to conditions to which he is accustomed and for which no exercise of the imagination is needed, unless we take the effect of memory to be, according to Queyrat, retrospective imagination.

The next incident that appeals is the unfamiliar

[1] This experiment cannot be made with a group of children for obvious reasons.

behavior of the toys, but still in familiar surroundings; that is to say, the *unusual* activities are carried on in the safe precincts of the nursery—the *usual* atmosphere of the child.

I quote from the text:

> Late in the evening the other soldiers were put in their box, and the people of the house went to bed. Now was the time for the toys to play; they amused themselves with paying visits, fighting battles and giving balls. The tin soldiers rustled about in their box, for they wanted to join the games, but they could not get the lid off. The nut-crackers turned somersaults, and the pencil scribbled nonsense on the slate.

Now, from this point onwards in the story, the events will be quite outside the personal experience of the child, and there will have to be a real stretch of imagination to appreciate the thrilling and blood-curdling adventures of the little tin soldier, namely, the terrible sailing down the gutter under the bridge, the meeting with the fierce rat who demands the soldier's passport, the horrible sensation in the fish's body, etc. Last of all, perhaps, will come the appreciation of the best qualities of the hero: his modesty, his dignity, his reticence, his courage and his constancy. He seems to combine all the qualities of the best soldier with those of the best civilian, without the more obvious qualities which generally attract first. As for the love story, we must not *expect* any child to see its tenderness and beauty, though the individual child may intuitively appreciate these qualities, but it is not what we wish for or work for at this period of child life.

This method could be applied to various stories. I have chosen the "Tin Soldier" because of its dramatic qualities and because it is marked off, probably quite unconsciously on the part of Andersen into periods which correspond to the child's development.

In Eugene Field's exquisite little poem of "The Dinkey Bird," we find the objects familiar to the child in *unusual* places, so that some imagination is needed to realize that "big red sugar-plums are clinging to the cliffs beside that sea"; but the introduction of the fantastic bird and the soothing sound of the amfalula tree are new and delightful sensations, quite out of the child's personal experience.

Another such instance is to be found in Mrs. W. K. Clifford's story of "Master Willie." The abnormal behavior of familiar objects, such as a doll, leads from the ordinary routine to the paths of adventure. This story is to be found in a little book called "Very Short Stories," a most interesting collection for teachers and children.

We now come to the second element we should seek in material, namely, the element of the unusual, which we have already anticipated in the story of the "Tin Soldier."

This element is necessary in response to the demand of the child who expressed the needs of his fellow-playmates when he said: "I want to go to the place where the shadows are real." This is the true definition of "faerie" lands and is the first sign of real mental development in the child when he is no longer content with the stories of his own little deeds and experiences, when his ear begins to appreciate sounds different from the words in his own everyday language, and when he begins to separate his own personality from the action of the story.

George Goschen says:

"What I want for the young are books and stories which do not simply deal with our daily life. I like the fancy even of little children to have some larger food than images of their own little lives, and I confess I am sorry for the children whose imaginations are not sometimes stimulated by beautiful fairy tales which carry them to worlds different from those in which their future will be passed. . . . I hold that what removes them more or less from their daily life is better than what reminds them of it at every step." [1]

It is because of the great value of leading children to something beyond the limited circle of their own lives that I deplore the twaddling boarding-school stories written for girls and the artificially

[1] From an address on "The Cultivation of the Imagination."

prepared public school stories for boys. Why not give them the dramatic interest of a larger stage? No account of a cricket match or a football triumph could present a finer appeal to boys and girls than the description of the Peacestead in the "Heroes of Asgaard":

"This was the playground of the Æsir, where they practiced trials of skill one with another and held tournaments and sham fights. These last were always conducted in the gentlest and most honorable manner; for the strongest law of the Peacestead was that no angry blow should be struck or spiteful word spoken upon the sacred field."

For my part, I would unhesitatingly give to boys and girls an element of strong romance in the stories which are told them even before they are twelve.

Miss Sewell says:

"The system that keeps girls in the schoolroom reading simple stories, without reading Scott and Shakespeare and Spenser, and then hands them over to the unexplored recesses of the Circulating Library, has been shown to be the most frivolizing that can be devised." She sets forth as the result of her experience that a good novel, especially a romantic one, read at twelve or fourteen, is really a beneficial thing.

At present, so many of the children from the elementary schools get their first idea of love, if one can give it such a name, from vulgar pictures displayed in the shop windows or jokes on marriage, culled from the lowest type of paper, or the proceedings of a divorce court.

What an antidote to such representation might be found in the stories of Hector and Andromache, Siegfried and Brünnehilde, Dido and Æneas, Orpheus and Eurydice, St. Francis and St. Clare!

One of the strongest elements we should introduce into our stories for children of all ages is that which calls forth love of beauty. And the beauty should stand out, not only in the delineation of noble qualities in our heroes and heroines, but in the beauty and strength of language and form.

In this latter respect, the Bible stories are of such inestimable value; all the greater because a child is familiar with the subject and the stories gain fresh significance from the spoken or winged word as compared with the mere reading. As to whether we should keep to the actual text is a matter of individual experience. Professor R. G. Moulton, whose interpretations of the Bible stories are so well known both in England and America, does not always confine himself to the actual text, but draws the dramatic elements together, rejecting what seems to him to break the narrative, but introducing the actual language where it is the most effective. Those who have heard him will realize the success of his method.

There is one Bible story which can be told with

scarcely any deviation from the text, if only a few hints are given beforehand, and that is the story of Nebuchadnezzar and the Golden Image. Thus, I think it wise, if the children are to succeed in partially visualizing the story, that they should have some idea of the dimensions of the Golden Image as it would stand out in a vast plain. It might be well to compare those dimensions with some building with which the child is familiar. In London, the matter is easy as the height will compare, roughly speaking, with Westminster Abbey. The only change in the text I should adopt is to avoid the constant enumeration of the list of rulers and the musical instruments. In doing this, I am aware that I am sacrificing something of beauty in the rhythm, but, on the other hand, for narrative purpose the interest is not broken. The first time the announcement is made, that is, by the Herald, it should be in a perfectly loud, clear and toneless voice, such as you would naturally use when shouting through a trumpet to a vast concourse of people scattered over a wide plain, reserving all the dramatic tone of voice for the passage where Nebuchadnezzar is making the announcement to the three men by themselves. I can remember Professor Moulton saying that all the dramatic interest of the story is summed up in the words "But if not . . ." This suggestion is a very helpful one, for it enables us to work up gradually to this point, and then, as it were, *unwind,* until we reach the words of Nebuchadnezzar's dramatic recantation.

In this connection, it is a good plan occasionally during the story hour to introduce really good poetry which, delivered in a dramatic manner (far removed, of course, from the melodramatic), might give children their first love of beautiful form in verse. And I do not think it necessary to wait for this. Even the normal child of seven, though there is nothing arbitrary in the suggestion of this age, will appreciate the effect, if only on the ear, of beautiful lines well spoken. Mahomet has said, in his teaching advice: "Teach your children poetry; it opens the mind, lends grace to wisdom and makes heroic virtues hereditary."

To begin with the youngest children of all, here is a poem which contains a thread of story, just enough to give a human interest:

MILKING-TIME

When the cows come home, the milk is coming;
Honey's made when the bees are humming.
Duck, drake on the rushy lake,
And the deer live safe in the breezy brake,
And timid, funny, pert little bunny
Winks his nose, and sits all sunny.

CHRISTINA ROSSETTI.

Now, in comparing this poem with some of the doggerel verse offered to small children, one is struck with the literary superiority in the choice of words. Here, in spite of the simplicity of the poem, there is not the ordinary limited vocabulary, nor the forced rhyme, nor the application of a moral, by which the artist falls from grace.

Again, Eugene Field's "Hushaby Lady," of which the language is most simple, yet the child is carried away by the beauty of the sound.

I remember hearing some poetry repeated by the children in one of the elementary schools in Sheffield which made me feel that they had realized romantic possibilities which would prevent their lives from ever becoming quite prosaic again, and I wish that this practice were more usual. There is little difficulty with the children. I can remember, in my own experience as a teacher in London, making the experiment of reading or repeating passages from Milton and Shakespeare to children from nine to eleven years of age, and the enthusiastic way they responded by learning those passages by heart. I have taken with several sets of children such passages from Milton as the "Echo Song," "Sabrina," "By the Rushy-fringed Bank," "Back, Shepherds, Back," from "Comus"; "May Morning," "Ode to Shakespeare," "Samson," "On His Blindness," etc. I even ventured on several passages from "Paradise Lost," and found "Now came still evening on" a particular favorite with the children.

It seemed even easier to interest them in Shakespeare, and they learned quite readily and easily many passages from "As You Like It," "The Merchant of Venice," "Julius Cæsar," "Richard II," "Henry IV," and "Henry V."

The method I should recommend in the introduction of both poets occasionally into the story-hour would be threefold. First, to choose passages which appeal for beauty of sound or beauty of mental vision called up by those sounds; such as "Tell me where is Fancy bred," "Titania's Lullaby," "How sweet the moonlight sleeps upon this bank." Secondly, passages for sheer interest of content, such as the Trial Scene from "The Merchant of Venice," or the Forest Scene in "As You Like It." Thirdly, for dramatic and historical interest, such as, "Men at some time are masters of their fates," the whole of Mark Antony's speech, and the scene with Imogen and her foster brothers in the Forest.

It may not be wholly out of place to add here that the children learned and repeated these passages themselves, and that I offered them the same advice as I do to all story-tellers. I discussed quite openly with them the method I considered best, trying to make them see that simplicity of delivery was not only the most beautiful but the most effective means to use and, by the end of a few months, when they had been allowed to experiment and express themselves, they began to see that mere ranting was not force and that a sense of reserve power is infinitely more impressive and inspiring than mere external presentation.

I encouraged them to criticize each other for the common good, and sometimes I read a few lines with overemphasis and too much gesture, which they were at liberty to point out that they might avoid the same error.

Excellent collections of poems for this purpose of narrative are: Mrs. P. A. Barnett's series of "Song and Story," published by Adam Black, and "The Posy Ring," chosen and classified by Kate Douglas Wiggin and Nora Archibald Smith, published by Doubleday. For older children, "The Call of the Homeland," selected and arranged by Dr. R. P. Scott and Katharine T. Wallas, published by Blackie; "A Book of Famous Verse," selected by Agnes Repplier, published by Houghton, Mifflin, and "Golden Numbers," chosen and classified by Kate Douglas Wiggin and Nora Archibald Smith, published by Doubleday.

I think it is well to have a goodly number of stories illustrating the importance of common-sense and resourcefulness.

For this reason, I consider the stories treating of the ultimate success of the youngest son[1] very admirable for the purpose, because the youngest child who begins by being considered inferior to the older

[1] "The House in the Wood" (Grimm), is another instance of triumph for the youngest child.

ones triumphs in the end, either from resourcefulness or from common-sense or from some higher quality, such as kindness to animals, courage in overcoming difficulties, etc.

Thus, we have the story of Cinderella. The cynic might imagine that it was the diminutive size of her foot that insured her success. The child does not realize any advantage in this, but, though the matter need not be pressed, the story leaves us with the impression that Cinderella had been patient and industrious, and forbearing with her sisters. We know that she was strictly obedient to her godmother, and in order to be this she makes her dramatic exit from the ball which is the beginning of her triumph. There are many who might say that these qualities do not meet with reward in life and that they end in establishing a habit of drudgery, but, after all, we must have poetic justice in a fairy story, occasionally, at any rate, even if the child is confused by the apparent contradiction.

Such a story is "Jesper and the Hares." Here, however, it is not at first resourcefulness that helps the hero, but sheer kindness of heart, which prompts him first to help the ants, and then to show civility to the old woman, without for a moment expecting any material benefit from such actions. At the end, he does win on his own ingenuity and resourcefulness, and if we regret that his trickery has such wonderful results, we must remember the aim was to win the princess for herself, and that there was little choice left him. I consider that the end of this story is one of the most remarkable I have found in my long years of browsing among fairy tales. I should suggest stopping at the words: "The Tub is full," as any addition seems to destroy the subtlety of the story.[1]

Another story of this kind, admirable for children from six years and upwards, is, "What the Old Man Does is Always Right." Here, perhaps, the entire lack of common-sense on the part of the hero would serve rather as a warning than a stimulating example, but the conduct of the wife in excusing the errors of her foolish husband is a model of resourcefulness.

In the story of "Hereafter-this," [2] we have just the converse: a perfectly foolish wife shielded by a most patient and forbearing husband, whose tolerance and common-sense save the situation.

One of the most important elements to seek in our choice of stories is that which tends to develop, eventually, a fine sense of humor in a child. I purposely use the word, "eventually," because I realize, first, that humor has various stages, and that seldom, if ever, can one expect an appreciation of fine humor from a normal child, that is, from an elemental

[1] To be found in Andrew Lang's "The Violet Fairy Book."
[2] To be found in Jacob's "More English Fairy Tales."

mind. It seems as if the rough-and-tumble element were almost a necessary stage through which children must pass, and which is a normal and healthy stage; but up to now we have quite unnecessarily extended the period of elephantine fun, and, though we cannot control the manner in which children are catered to along this line in their homes, we can restrict the folly of appealing too strongly or too long to this elemental faculty in our schools. Of course, the temptation is strong because the appeal is so easy, but there is a tacit recognition that horseplay and practical jokes are no longer considered as an essential part of a child's education. We note this in the changed attitude in the schools, taken by more advanced educators, towards bullying, fagging, hazing, etc. As a reaction, then, from more obvious fun, there should be a certain number of stories which make appeal to a more subtle element, and in the chapter on the questions put to me by teachers on various occasions I speak more in detail as to the educational value of a finer humor in our stories.

At some period there ought to be presented in our stories the superstitions connected with the primitive history of the race, dealing with the fairy proper, giants, dwarfs, gnomes, nixies, brownies and other elemental beings. Andrew Lang says: "Without our savage ancestors we should have had no poetry. Conceive the human race born into the world in its present advanced condition, weighing, analyzing, examining everything. Such a race would have been destitute of poetry and flattened by common-sense. Barbarians did the *dreaming* of the world."

But it is a question of much debate among educators as to what should be the period of the child's life in which these stories are to be presented. I, myself, was formerly of the opinion that they belonged to the very primitive age of the individual, just as they belong to the primitive age of the race, but experience in telling stories has taught me to compromise.

Some people maintain that little children, who take things with brutal logic, ought not to be allowed the fairy tale in its more limited form of the supernatural; whereas, if presented to older children, this material can be criticized, catalogued and (alas!) rejected as worthless, or retained with flippant toleration.

While realizing a certain value in this point of view, I am bound to admit that if we regulate our stories entirely on this basis, we lose the real value of the fairy tale element. It is the one element which causes little children to *wonder,* simply because no scientific analysis of the story can be presented to them. It is somewhat heartrending to feel that "Jack and the Bean Stalk" and stories of that ilk are to be handed over to the critical youth who will condemn the quick growth of the tree as being contrary to the order of nature, and wonder why *Jack* was not playing football on the school team instead of climbing trees in search of imaginary adventures.

A wonderful plea for the telling of early superstitions to children is to be found in an old Indian allegory called, "The Blazing Mansion."

An old man owned a large rambling Mansion. The pillars were rotten, the galleries tumbling down, the thatch dry and combustible, and there was only one door. Suddenly, one day, there was a smell of fire: the old man rushed out. To his horror he saw that the thatch was aflame, the rotten pillars were catching fire one by one, and the rafters were burning like tinder. But, inside, the children went on amusing themselves quite happily. The distracted Father said: "I will run in and save my children. I will seize them in my strong arms, I will bear them harmless through the falling rafters and the blazing beams." Then the sad thought came to him that the children were romping and ignorant. "If I say the house is on fire, they will not understand me. If I try to seize them, they will romp about and try to escape. Alas! not a moment to be lost!" Suddenly a bright thought flashed across the old man's mind. "My children are ignorant," he said; "they love toys and glittering playthings. I will promise them playthings of unheard-of beauty. Then they will listen."

So the old man shouted: "Children, come out of the house and see these beautiful toys! Chariots with white oxen, all gold and tinsel. See these exquisite little antelopes. Whoever saw such goats as these? Children, children, come quickly, or they will all be gone!"

Forth from the blazing ruin the children came in hot

> haste. The word, "plaything," was almost the only word they could understand.
>
> Then the Father, rejoiced that his offspring were freed from peril, procured for them one of the most beautiful chariots ever seen. The chariot had a canopy like a pagoda; it had tiny rails and balustrades and rows of jingling bells. Milk-white oxen drew the chariot. The children were astonished when they were placed inside.[1]

Perhaps, as a compromise, one might give the gentler superstitions to very small children, and leave such a blood-curdling story as "Bluebeard" to a more robust age.

There is one modern method which has always seemed to me much to be condemned, and that is the habit of changing the end of a story, for fear of alarming the child. This is quite indefensible. In doing this we are tampering with folklore and confusing stages of development.

Now, I know that there are individual children that, at a tender age, might be alarmed at such a story, for instance, as "Little Red Riding-Hood"; in which case, it is better to sacrifice the "wonder stage" and present the story later on.

I live in dread of finding one day a bowdlerized form of "Bluebeard," prepared for a junior standard, in which, to produce a satisfactory finale, all the wives come to life again, and "live happily forever after" with Bluebeard and each other!

And from this point it seems an easy transition to

[1] From the "Thabagata."

the subject of legends of different kinds. Some of the old country legends in connection with flowers are very charming for children, and so long as we do not tread on the sacred ground of the nature students, we may indulge in a moderate use of such stories, of which a few will be found in the List of Stories, given later.

With regard to the introduction of legends connected with saints into the school curriculum, my chief plea is the element of the unusual which they contain and an appeal to a sense of mysticism and wonder which is a wise antidote to the prosaic and commercial tendencies of today. Though many of the actions of the saints may be the result of a morbid strain of self-sacrifice, at least none of them was engaged in the sole occupation of becoming rich: their ideals were often lofty and unselfish; their courage high, and their deeds noble. We must be careful, in the choice of our legends, to show up the virile qualities rather than to dwell on the elements of horror in details of martyrdom, or on the too-constantly recurring miracles, lest we should defeat our own ends. For the children might think lightly of the dangers to which the saints were exposed if they find them too often preserved at the last moment from the punishment they were brave enough to undergo. For one or another of these reasons, I should avoid the detailed history of St. Juliana, St. Vincent, St. Quintin, St. Eustace, St.

Winifred, St. Theodore, St. James the More, St. Katharine, St. Cuthbert, St. Alphage, St. Peter of Milan, St. Quirine and Juliet, St. Alban and others.

The danger of telling children stories connected with sudden conversions is that they are apt to place too much emphasis on the process, rather than on the goal to be reached. We should always insist on the splendid deeds performed after a real conversion, not the details of the conversion itself; as, for instance, the beautiful and poetical work done by St. Christopher when he realized what work he could do most effectively.

On the other hand, there are many stories of the saints dealing with actions and motives which would appeal to the imagination and are not only worthy of imitation, but are not wholly outside the life and experience even of the child.[1]

Having protested against the elephantine joke and the too-frequent use of exaggerated fun, I now endeavor to restore the balance by suggesting the introduction into the school curriculum of a few purely grotesque stories which serve as an antidote to sentimentality or utilitarianism. But they must be presented as nonsense, so that the children may use them for what they are intended as—pure relaxation. Such a story is that of "The Wolf and the Kids,"

[1] For selection of suitable stories among legends of the Saints, see list of stories under the heading, "Stories of the Saints." The *Legenda Aurea* (Temple Classics) is a rich storehouse.

which I present in my own version to children and adults. I have had serious objections offered to this story by several educational people, because of the revenge taken by the goat on the wolf, but I am inclined to think that if the story is to be taken as anything but sheer nonsense, it is surely sentimental to extend our sympathy towards a caller who has devoured six of his hostess' children. With regard to the wolf being cut open, there is not the slightest need to accentuate the physical side. Children accept the deed as they accept the cutting off of a giant's head, because they do not associate it with pain, especially if the deed is presented half humorously. The moment in the story where their sympathy is aroused is the swallowing of the kids, because the children do realize the possibility of being disposed of in the mother's absence. (Needless to say, I never point out the moral of the kids' disobedience to the mother in opening the door.) I have always noticed a moment of breathlessness even in a grown-up audience when the wolf swallows the kids, and that the recovery of them "all safe and sound, all huddled together" is quite as much appreciated by the adult audience as by the children, and is worth the tremor caused by the wolf's summary action.

I have not always been able to impress upon the teachers the fact that this story *must* be taken lightly. A very earnest young student came to me once after the telling of this story and said in an awe-struck voice: "Do you cor-relate?" Having recovered from the effect of this word, which she carefully explained, I said that, as a rule, I preferred to keep the story quite apart from the other lessons, just an undivided whole, because it had effects of its own which were best brought about by not being connected with other lessons. She frowned her disapproval and said: "I am sorry, because I thought I would take the Goat for my nature study lesson, and then tell your story at the end." I thought of the terrible struggle in the child's mind between his conscientious wish to be accurate and his dramatic enjoyment of the abnormal habits of a goat who went out with scissors, needle and thread; but I have been most careful since to repudiate any connection with nature study in this and a few other stories in my répertoire.

One might occasionally introduce one of Edward Lear's "Nonsense Rhymes." For instance:

> There was an Old Man of Cape Horn
> Who wished he had never been born.
>   So he sat in a chair
>   Till he died of despair,
> That dolorous Old Man of Cape Horn.

Now, except in case of very young children, this could not possibly be taken seriously. The least observant normal boy or girl would recognize the hollowness of the pessimism that prevents an old man from at least an attempt to rise from his chair.

The following I have chosen as repeated with intense appreciation and much dramatic vigor by a little boy just five years old:

> There was an old man who said: "Hush!
> I perceive a young bird in that bush."
> When they said: "Is it small?"
> He replied, "Not at all.
> It is four times as large as the bush." [1]

One of the most desirable of all elements to introduce into our stories is that which encourages kinship with animals. With very young children this is easy, because during those early years when the mind is not clogged with knowledge, the sympathetic imagination enables them to enter into the feelings of animals. Andersen has an illustration of this point in his "Ice Maiden":

"Children who cannot talk yet can understand the language of fowls and ducks quite well, and cats and dogs speak to them quite as plainly as Father and Mother; but that is only when the children are very small, and then even Grandpapa's stick will become a perfect horse to them that can neigh and, in their eyes, is furnished with legs and a tail. With some children this period ends later than with others, and of such we are accustomed to say that they are very backward, and that they have remained

[1] These words have been set most effectively to music by Miss Margaret Ruthven Lang.

children for a long time. People are in the habit of saying strange things."

Felix Adler says:

"Perhaps the chief attraction of fairy tales is due to their representing the child as living in brotherly friendship with nature and all creatures. Trees, flowers, animals, wild and tame, even the stars are represented as comrades of children. That animals are only human beings in disguise is an axiom in the fairy tales. Animals are humanized, that is, the kinship between animal and human life is still keenly felt, and this reminds us of those early animistic interpretations of nature which subsequently led to doctrines of metempsychosis." [1]

I think that beyond question the finest animal stories are to be found in the Indian collections, of which I furnish a list in the last chapter.

With regard to the development of the love of Nature through the telling of stories, we are confronted with a great difficulty in the elementary schools because so many of the children have never been out of the towns, have never seen a daisy, a blade of grass and scarcely a tree, so that in giving, in the form of a story, a beautiful description of scenery, you can make no appeal to the retrospective imagination, and only the rarely gifted child will be able to make pictures while listening to a style which

[1] From "The Use of Fairy Tales," in "Moral Instruction of Children."

is beyond his everyday use. Nevertheless, once in a while, when the children are in a quiet mood, not eager for action but able to give themselves up to the pure joy of sound, then it is possible to give them a beautiful piece of writing in praise of Nature, such as the following, taken from "The Divine Adventure," by Fiona Macleod:

> Then he remembered the ancient wisdom of the Gael and came out of the Forest Chapel and went into the woods. He put his lip to the earth, and lifted a green leaf to his brow, and held a branch to his ear; and because he was no longer heavy with the sweet clay of mortality, though yet of human clan, he heard that which we do not hear, and saw that which we do not see, and knew that which we do not know. All the green life was his. In that new world he saw the lives of trees, now pale green, now of woodsmoke blue, now of amethyst; the gray lives of stone; breaths of the grass and reed, creatures of the air, delicate and wild as fawns, or swift and fierce and terrible tigers of that undiscovered wilderness, with birds almost invisible but for their luminous wings, and opalescent crests.

The value of this particular passage is the mystery pervading the whole picture, which forms so beautiful an antidote to the eternal explaining of things. I think it of the highest importance for children to realize that the best and most beautiful things cannot be expressed in everyday language and that they must content themselves with a flash here and there of the beauty which may come later. One does not enhance the beauty of the mountain by pulling to pieces some of the earthy clogs; one does not increase the impression of a vast ocean by analyzing the single drops of water. But at a reverent distance one gets a clear impression of the whole, and can afford to leave the details in the shadow.

In presenting such passages (and it must be done very sparingly), experience has taught me that we should take the children into our confidence by telling them frankly that nothing exciting is going to happen, so that they will be free to listen to the mere words. A very interesting experiment might occasionally be made by asking the children some weeks afterwards to tell you in their own words what pictures were made on their minds. This is a very different thing from allowing the children to reproduce the passage at once, the danger of which proceeding I speak of later in detail.[1]

We now come to the question as to what proportion of *dramatic excitement* we should present in the stories for a normal group of children. Personally, I should like, while the child is very young, I mean in mind, not in years, to exclude the element of dramatic excitement, but though this may be possible for the individual child, it is quite Utopian to hope that we can keep the average child free from what is in the atmosphere. Children crave for excitement, and unless we give it to them in legitimate

[1] See Chapter on Questions asked by Teachers.

form, they will take it in any riotous form it presents itself, and if from our experience we can control their mental digestion by a moderate supply of what they demand, we may save them from devouring too eagerly the raw material they can so easily find for themselves.

There is a humorous passage bearing on this question in the story of the small Scotch boy, when he asks leave of his parents to present the pious little book—a gift to himself from an aunt to a little sick friend, hoping probably that the friend's chastened condition will make him more lenient towards this mawkish form of literature. The parents expostulate, pointing out to their son how ungrateful he is, and how ungracious it would be to part with his aunt's gift. Then the boy can contain himself no longer. He bursts out, unconsciously expressing the normal attitude of children at a certain stage of development:

> "It's a *daft* book ony way: there's naebody gets kilt ent. I like stories about folk gettin' their heids cut off, or stabbit, through and through, wi' swords an' spears. An' there's nae wile beasts. I like stories about black men gettin' ate up, an' white men killin' lions and tigers an' bears an'——"

Then, again, we have the passage from George Eliot's "Mill on the Floss":

> "Oh, dear! I wish they would not fight at your school, Tom. Didn't it hurt you?"

"Hurt me? No," said Tom, putting up the hooks again, taking out a large pocketknife, and slowly opening the largest blade, which he looked at meditatively as he rubbed his finger along it. Then he added:

"I gave Spooner a black eye—that's what he got for wanting to leather me. I wasn't going to go halves because anybody leathered me."

"Oh! how brave you are, Tom. I think you are like Samson. If there came a lion roaring at me, I think you'd fight him, wouldn't you, Tom?"

"How can a lion come roaring at you, you silly thing? There's no lions only in the shows."

"No, but if we were in the lion countries—I mean in Africa where it's very hot, the lions eat people there. I can show it you in the book where I read it."

"Well, I should get a gun and shoot him."

"But if you hadn't got a gun?—we might have gone out, you know, not thinking, just as we go out fishing, and then a great lion might come towards us roaring, and we could not get away from him. What should you do, Tom?"

Tom paused, and at last turned away contemptuously, saying: "But the lion *isn't* coming. What's the use of talking?"

This passage illustrates also the difference between the highly-developed imagination of the one and the stodgy prosaical temperament of the other. Tom could enter into the elementary question of giving his schoolfellow a black eye, but could not possibly enter into the drama of the imaginary arrival of a lion. He was sorely in need of fairy stories.

It is to this element we have to cater, and we cannot shirk our responsibilities.

William James says:

"Living things, moving things or things that savor of danger or blood, that have a dramatic quality, these are the things natively interesting to childhood, to the exclusion of almost everything else, and the teacher of young children, until more artificial interests have grown up, will keep in touch with his pupils by constant appeal to such matters as these."[1]

Of course the savor of danger and blood is only *one* of the things to which we should appeal, but I give the whole passage to make the point clearer.

This is one of the most difficult parts of our selection, namely, how to present enough excitement for the child and yet include enough constructive element which will satisfy him when the thirst for "blugginess" is slaked.

And here I should like to say that, while wishing to encourage in children great admiration and reverence for the courage and other fine qualities which have been displayed in times of war and which have mitigated its horrors, I think we should show that some of the finest moments in these heroes' lives had nothing to do with their profession as soldiers. Thus, we have the well-known story of Sir Philip Sydney and the soldier; the wonderful scene where Roland drags the bodies of his dead friends to re-

[1] From "Talks to Teachers," page 93.

ceive the blessing of the Archbishop after the battle of Roncesvalle;[1] and of Napoleon sending the sailor back to England. There is a moment in the story of Gunnar when he pauses in the midst of the slaughter of his enemies, and says, "I wonder if I am less base than others, because I kill men less willingly than they."

And in the "Burning of Njal,"[2] we have the words of the boy, Thord, when his grandmother, Bergthora, urges him to go out of the burning house.

"'You promised me when I was little, grandmother, that I should never go from you till I wished it of myself. And I would rather die with you than live after you.'"

Here the moral courage is so splendidly shown: none of these heroes feared to die in battle or in open single fight; but to face a death by fire for higher considerations is a point of view worth presenting to the child.

In spite of all the dramatic excitement roused by the conduct of our soldiers and sailors, should we not try to offer also in our stories the romance and excitement of saving as well as taking life?

I would have quite a collection dealing with the

---

[1] An excellent account of this is to be found in "The Song of Roland," by Arthur Way and Frederic Spender.

[2] Njal's Burning, from "The Red Book of Romance," by Andrew Lang.

thrilling adventures of the Lifeboat and the Fire Brigade, of which I shall present examples in the final story list.

Finally, we ought to include a certain number of stories dealing with death, especially with children who are of an age to realize that it must come to all, and that this is not a calamity but a perfectly natural and simple thing. At present the child in the street invariably connects death with sordid accidents. I think they should have stories of death coming in heroic form, as when a man or woman dies for a great cause, in which he has opportunity of admiring courage, devotion and unselfishness; or of death coming as a result of treachery, such as we find in the death of Baldur, the death of Siegfried, and others, so that children may learn to abhor such deeds; but also a fair proportion of stories dealing with death that comes naturally, when our work is done, and our strength gone, which has no more tragedy than the falling of a leaf from the tree. In this way, we can give children the first idea that the individual is so much less than the whole.

Little children often take death very naturally. A boy of five met two of his older companions at the school door. They said sadly and solemnly: "We have just seen a dead man!" "Well," said the little philosopher, "that's all right. We've *all* got to die when our work's done."

In one of the Buddha stories which I reproduce

at the end of this book, the little Hare (who is, I think, a symbol of nervous individualism) constantly says: "Suppose the Earth were to fall in, what would become of me?"

As an antidote to the ordinary attitude towards death, I commend an episode from a German folk-lore story which is called "Unlucky John," and which is included in the list of stories recommended at the end of this book.

The following sums up in poetic form some of the material necessary for the wants of a child.

THE CHILD

1

The little new soul has come to earth,
He has taken his staff for the Pilgrim's way.
His sandals are girt on his tender feet,
And he carries his scrip for what gifts he may.

2

What will you give to him, Fate Divine?
What for his scrip on the winding road?
A crown for his head, or a laurel wreath?
A sword to wield, or is gold his load?

3

What will you give him for weal or woe?
What for the journey through day and night?
Give or withhold from him power and fame,
But give to him love of the earth's delight.

4

Let him be lover of wind and sun
  And of falling rain; and the friend of trees;
With a singing heart for the pride of noon,
  And a tender heart for what twilight sees.

5

Let him be lover of you and yours—
  The Child and Mary; but also Pan
And the sylvan gods of the woods and hills,
  And the god that is hid in his fellowman.

6

Love and a song and the joy of earth,
  These be the gifts for his scrip to keep
Till, the journey ended, he stands at last
  In the gathering dark, at the gate of sleep.

ETHEL CLIFFORD.

And so our stories should contain all the essentials for the child's scrip on the road of life, providing the essentials and holding or withholding the non-essentials. But, above all, let us fill the scrip with gifts that the child need never reject, even when he passes through to "the gate of sleep."

CHAPTER VI

HOW TO OBTAIN AND MAINTAIN THE EFFECT OF THE STORY

We are now come to the most important part of the question of story-telling, to which all the foregoing remarks have been gradually leading, and that is the effect of these stories upon the child, quite apart from the dramatic joy he experiences in listening to them, which would in itself be quite enough to justify us in the telling. But, since I have urged the extreme importance of giving so much time to the manner of telling and of bestowing so much care in the selection of the material, it is right that we should expect some permanent results or else those who are not satisfied with the mere enjoyment of the children will seek other methods of appeal—and it is to them that I most specially dedicate this chapter.

I think we are on the threshold of the re-discovery of an old truth, that *dramatic presentation* is the quickest and the surest method of appeal, because it is the only one with which memory plays no tricks. If a thing has appeared before us in a vital form, nothing can really destroy it; it is because things are often given in a blurred, faint light that they gradually fade out of our memory. A very keen scientist was deploring to me, on one occasion, the fact that stories were told so much in the schools, to the detriment of science, for which she claimed the same indestructible element that I recognize in the best-told stories. Being very much interested in her point of view, I asked her to tell me, looking back on her school days, what she could remember as standing out from other less clear information. After thinking some little time over the matter, she said with some embarrassment, but with a candor that did her much honor:

"Well, now I come to think of it, it was the story of Cinderella."

Now, I am not holding any brief for this story in particular. I think the reason it was remembered was because of the dramatic form in which it was presented to her, which fired her imagination and kept the memory alight. I quite realize that a scientific fact might also have been easily remembered if it had been presented in the form of a successful chemical experiment; but this also has something of the dramatic appeal and will be remembered on that account.

Sully says: "We cannot understand the fascination of a story for children save in remembering that for their young minds, quick to imagine, and unversed in abstract reflection, words are not dead things but *winged,* as the old Greeks called them."[1]

The *Red Queen,* in "Alice Through the Looking-Glass," was more psychological than she was aware of when she made the memorable statement: "When once you've *said* a thing, that *fixes* it, and you must take the consequences."

In Curtin's "Introduction to Myths and Folk Tales of the Russians," he says:

"I remember well the feelings roused in my mind at the mention or sight of the name *Lucifer* during the early years of my life. It stood for me as the name of a being stupendous, dreadful in moral deformity, lurid, hideous and mighty. I remember the surprise with which, when I had grown somewhat older and began to study Latin, I came upon the name in Virgil where it means *light-bringer*—the herald of the Sun."

Plato has said that "the end of education should be the training by suitable habits of the instincts of virtue in the child."

About two thousand years later, Sir Philip Sydney, in his "Defence of Poesy," says: "The final end of learning is to draw and lead us to so high a perfection as our degenerate souls, made worse by their clay lodgings, can be capable of."

And yet it is neither the Greek philosopher nor the Elizabethan poet that makes the everyday appli-

[1] From "Studies of Childhood."

cation of these principles; but we have a hint of this application from the Pueblo tribe of Indians, of whom Lummis tells us the following:

"There is no duty to which a Pueblo child is trained in which he has to be content with a bare command: do this. For each, he learns a fairy-tale designed to explain how children first came to know that it was right to 'do this,' and detailing the sad results that befell those who did otherwise. Some tribes have regular story-tellers, men who have devoted a great deal of time to learning the myths and stories of their people and who possess, in addition to a good memory, a vivid imagination. The mother sends for one of these, and having prepared a feast for him, she and her little brood, who are curled up near her, await the fairy stories of the dreamer, who after his feast and smoke entertains the company for hours."

In modern times, the nurse, who is now receiving such complete training for her duties with children, should be ready to imitate the "dreamer" of the Indian tribe. I rejoice to find that regular instruction in story-telling is being given in many of the institutions where the nurses are trained.

Some years ago there appeared a book by Dion Calthrop called "King Peter," which illustrates very fully the effect of story-telling. It is the account of the education of a young prince which is carried on at first by means of stories, and later he is taken out into the arena of life to show what is happening there—the dramatic appeal being always the means used to awaken his imagination. The fact that only *one* story a year is told him prevents our seeing the effect from day to day, but the time matters little. We only need faith to believe that the growth, though slow, was sure.

There is something of the same idea in the "Adventures of Telemachus," written by Fénélon for his royal pupil, the young Duke of Burgundy, but whereas Calthrop trusts to the results of indirect teaching by means of dramatic stories, Fénélon, on the contrary, makes use of the somewhat heavy, didactic method, so that one would think the attention of the young prince must have wandered at times; and I imagine Telemachus was in the same condition when he was addressed at such length by Mentor, who, being Minerva, though in disguise, should occasionally have displayed that sense of humor which must always temper true wisdom.

Take, for instance, the heavy reproof conveyed in the following passage:

"Death and shipwreck are less dreadful than the pleasures that attack Virtue. . . . Youth is full of presumption and arrogance, though nothing in the world is so frail: it fears nothing, and vainly relies on its own strength, believing everything with the utmost levity and without any precaution."

And on another occasion, when Calypso hospitably provides clothes for the shipwrecked men, and Telemachus is handling a tunic of the finest wool and white as snow, with a vest of purple embroidered with gold, and displaying much pleasure in the magnificence of the clothes, Mentor addresses him in a severe voice, saying: "Are these, O Telemachus, the thoughts that ought to occupy the heart of the son of Ulysses? A young man who loves to dress vainly, as a woman does, is unworthy of wisdom or glory."

I remember, as a schoolgirl of thirteen, having to commit to memory several books of these adventures, so as to become familiar with the style. Far from being impressed by the wisdom of Mentor, I was simply bored, and wondered why Telemachus did not escape from him. The only part in the book that really interested me was Calypso's unrequited love for Telemachus, but this was always the point where we ceased to learn by heart, which surprised me greatly, for it was here that the real human interest seemed to begin.

Of all the effects which I hope for from the telling of stories in the schools, I, personally, place first the dramatic joy we bring to the children and to ourselves. But there are many who would consider this result as fantastic, if not frivolous, and not to be classed among the educational values connected with the introduction of stories into the school curriculum. I, therefore, propose to speak of other effects of story-telling which may seem of more practical value.

The first, which is of a purely negative character, is that through means of a dramatic story we may counteract some of the sights and sounds of the streets which appeal to the melodramatic instinct in children. I am sure that all teachers whose work lies in crowded cities must have realized the effect produced on children by what they see and hear on their way to and from school. If we merely consider the bill boards with their realistic representations, quite apart from the actual dramatic happenings in the street, we at once perceive that the ordinary school interests pale before such lurid appeals as these. How can we expect the child who has stood openmouthed before a poster representing a woman chloroformed by a burglar (while that hero escapes in safety with her jewels) to display any interest in the arid monotony of the multiplication table? The illegitimate excitement created by the sight of the depraved burglar can only be counteracted by something equally exciting along the realistic but legitimate side of appeal; and this is where the story of the right kind becomes so valuable, and why the teacher who is artistic enough to undertake the task can find the short path to results which theorists seek for so long in vain. It is not even necessary to have an exceedingly exciting story;

sometimes one which will bring about pure reaction may be just as suitable.

I remember in my personal experience an instance of this kind. I had been reading with some children of about ten years old the story from "Cymbeline" of *Imogen* in the forest scene, when the brothers strew flowers upon her, and sing the funeral dirge,

> Fear no more the heat of the sun.

Just as we had all taken on this tender, gentle mood, the door opened and one of the prefects announced in a loud voice the news of the relief of Mafeking. The children were on their feet at once, cheering lustily, and for the moment the joy over the relief of the brave garrison was the predominant feeling. Then, before the jingo spirit had time to assert itself, I took advantage of a momentary reaction and said: "Now, children, don't you think we can pay England the tribute of going back to England's greatest poet?" In a few minutes we were back in the heart of the forest, and I can still hear the delightful intonation of those subdued voices repeating,

> Golden lads and girls all must
> Like chimney-sweepers come to dust.

It is interesting to note that the same problem that is exercising us today was a source of difficulty to people in remote times. The following is taken from an old Chinese document, and has particular interest for us at this time:

"The philosopher, Mentius (born 371 B. C.), was left fatherless at a very tender age and brought up by his mother, Changsi. The care of this prudent and attentive mother has been cited as a model for all virtuous parents. The house she occupied was near that of a butcher; she observed at the first cry of the animals that were being slaughtered, the little Mentius ran to be present at the sight, and that, on his return, he sought to imitate what he had seen. Fearful lest his heart might become hardened, and accustomed to the sights of blood, she removed to another house which was in the neighborhood of a cemetery. The relations of those who were buried there came often to weep upon their graves, and make their customary libations. The lad soon took pleasure in their ceremonies and amused himself by imitating them. This was a new subject of uneasiness to his mother: she feared her son might come to consider as a jest what is of all things the most serious, and that he might acquire a habit of performing with levity, and as a matter of routine merely, ceremonies which demand the most exact attention and respect. Again, therefore, she anxiously changed the dwelling, and went to live in the city, opposite to a school, where her son found examples the most worthy of imitation, and began to profit by them. This anecdote has become incorporated by the Chinese into a proverb, which they constantly quote: The mother of Mentius seeks a neighborhood."

Another influence we have to counteract is that of newspaper headings and placards which catch the eye of children in the streets and appeal so powerfully to their imagination.

Shakespeare has said:

> Tell me where is Fancy bred,
> Or in the heart, or in the head?
> How begot, how nourished?
> It is engendered in the eyes
> With gazing fed,
> And Fancy dies in the cradle where it lies.
> Let us all ring Fancy's knell.
> I'll begin it—ding, dong, bell.
>
> —*The Merchant of Venice.*

If this be true, it is of importance to decide what our children shall look upon as far as we can control the vision, so that we can form some idea of the effect upon their imagination.

Having alluded to the dangerous influence of the street, I should hasten to say that this influence is very far from being altogether bad. There are possibilities of romance in street life which may have just the same kind of effect on children as the telling of exciting stories. I am indebted to Mrs. Arnold Glover, Honorary Secretary of the National Organization of Girls' Clubs,[1] one of the most

[1] England.

widely informed people on this subject, for the two following experiences gathered from the streets and which bear indirectly on the subject of story-telling:

Mrs. Glover was visiting a sick woman in a very poor neighborhood, and found, sitting on the door-step of the house, two little children, holding something tightly grasped in their little hands, and gazing with much expectancy towards the top of the street. She longed to know what they were doing, but not being one of those unimaginative and tactless folk who rush headlong into the mysteries of children's doings, she passed them at first in silence. It was only when she found them still in the same silent and expectant posture half an hour later that she said tentatively: "I wonder whether you would tell me what you are doing here?" After some hesitation, one of them said, in a shy voice: "We're waitin' for the barrer." It then transpired that, once a week, a vegetable- and flower-cart was driven through this particular street, on its way to a more prosperous neighborhood, and on a few red-letter days, a flower, or a sprig, or even a root sometimes fell out of the back of the cart; and these two little children were sitting there in hope, with their hands full of soil, ready to plant anything which might by some golden chance fall that way, in their secret garden of oyster shells.

This seems to me as charming a fairy tale as any that our books can supply.

On another occasion, Mrs. Glover was collecting the pennies for the Holiday Fund Savings Bank from the children who came weekly to her house. She noticed on three consecutive Mondays that one little lad deliberately helped himself to a new envelope from her table. Not wishing to frighten or startle him, she allowed this to continue for some weeks, and then one day, having dismissed the other children, she asked him quite quietly why he was taking the envelopes. At first he was very sulky, and said: "I need them more than you do." She quite agreed this might be, but reminded him that, after all, they belonged to her. She promised, however, that if he would tell her for what purpose he wanted the envelopes, she would endeavor to help him in the matter. Then came the astonishing announcement: "I am building a navy." After a little more gradual questioning, Mrs. Glover drew from the boy the information that the Borough water carts passed through the side street once a week, flushing the gutter; that then the envelope ships were made to sail on the water and pass under the covered ways which formed bridges for wayfarers and tunnels for the "navy." Great was the excitement when the ships passed out of sight and were recognized as they arrived safely at the other end. Of course, the expenses in raw material were greatly diminished by the illicit acquisition of Mrs. Glover's property, and in this way she had unconsciously provided the neighborhood with a navy and a commander. Her first instinct, after becoming acquainted with the whole story, was to present the boy with a real boat, but on second thought she collected and gave him a number of old envelopes with names and addresses upon them, which added greatly to the excitement of the sailing, because they could be more easily identified as they came out of the other end of the tunnel, and had their respective reputations as to speed.

Here is indeed food for romance, and I give both instances to prove that the advantages of street life are to be taken into consideration as well as the disadvantages, though I think we are bound to admit that the latter outweigh the former.

One of the immediate results of dramatic stories is the escape from the commonplace, to which I have already alluded in quoting Mr. Goschen's words. The desire for this escape is a healthy one, common to adults and children. When we wish to get away from our own surroundings and interests, we do for ourselves what I maintain we ought to do for children: we step into the land of fiction. It has always been a source of astonishment to me that, in trying to escape from our own everyday surroundings, we do not step more boldly into the land of pure romance, which would form a real contrast to our everyday life, but, in nine cases out of ten, the fiction which is sought after deals with the subjects of our ordinary existence, namely, frenzied finance, sordid poverty, political corruption, fast society, and religious doubts.

There is the same danger in the selection of fiction for children: namely, a tendency to choose very utilitarian stories, both in form and substance, so that we do not lift the children out of the commonplace. I remember once seeing the titles of two little books, the contents of which were being read or told to children; one was called, "Tom the Bootblack"; the other, "Dan the Newsboy." My chief objection to these stories was the fact that neither of the heroes rejoiced in his work for the work's sake. Had *Tom* even invented a new kind of blacking, or if *Dan* had started a newspaper, it might have been encouraging for those among the listeners who were thinking of engaging in similar professions. It is true, both gentlemen amassed large fortunes, but surely the school age is not to be limited to such dreams and aspirations as these! One wearies of the tales of boys who arrive in a town with one cent in their pocket and leave it as millionaires, with the added importance of a mayoralty. It is undoubtedly true that the romantic prototype of these worthy youths is *Dick Whittington,* for whom we unconsciously cherish the affection which we often bestow on a far-off personage. Perhaps—who can say?—it is the picturesque adjunct of the cat, lacking to modern millionaires.

I do not think it Utopian to present to children a fair share of stories which deal with the importance of things "untouched by hand." They, too, can learn at an early age that "the things which are seen are temporal, but the things which are unseen are spiritual." To those who wish to try the effect of such stories on children, I present for their encouragement the following lines from James Whitcomb Riley:

THE TREASURE OF THE WISE MAN [1]

Oh, the night was dark and the night was late,
When the robbers came to rob him;
And they picked the lock of his palace-gate,
The robbers who came to rob him—
They picked the lock of the palace-gate,
Seized his jewels and gems of State,
His coffers of gold and his priceless plate,—
The robbers that came to rob him.

But loud laughed he in the morning red!—
For of what had the robbers robbed him?
Ho! hidden safe, as he slept in bed,
When the robbers came to rob him,—
They robbed him not of a golden shred
Of the childish dreams in his wise old head—
"And they're welcome to all things else," he said,
When the robbers came to rob him.

---

[1] From "The Lockerbie Book," by James Whitcomb Riley, copyright, 1911. Used by special permission of the publishers, The Bobbs-Merrill Company.

There is a great deal of this romantic spirit, combined with a delightful sense of irresponsibility, which I claim above all things for small children, to be found in our old nursery rhymes. I quote from the following article written by the Rev. R. L. Gales for the *Nation*.

After speaking on the subject of fairy stories being eliminated from the school curriculum, the writer adds:

"This would be lessening the joy of the world and taking from generations yet unborn the capacity for wonder, the power to take a large unselfish interest in the spectacle of things, and putting them forever at the mercy of small private cares.

"A nursery rhyme is the most sane, the most unselfish thing in the world. It calls up some delightful image—a little nut-tree with a silver walnut and a golden pear; some romantic adventure only for the child's delight and liberation from the bondage of unseeing dullness: it brings before the mind the quintessence of some good thing:

" 'The little dog laughed to see such sport'—there is the soul of good humor, of sanity, of health in the laughter of that innocently wicked little dog. It is the laughter of pure frolic without unkindness. To have laughed with the little dog as a child is the best preservative against mirthless laughter in later years—the horse laughter of brutality, the ugly laughter of spite, the acrid laughter of fanaticism.

The world of nursery rhymes, the old world of Mrs. Slipper-Slopper, is the world of natural things, of quick, healthy motion, of the joy of living.

"In nursery rhymes the child is entertained with all the pageant of the world. It walks in fairy gardens, and for it the singing birds pass. All the King's horses and all the King's men pass before it in their glorious array. Craftsmen of all sorts, bakers, confectioners, silversmiths, blacksmiths are busy for it with all their arts and mysteries, as at the court of an eastern King."

In insisting upon the value of this escape from the commonplace, I cannot prove the importance of it more clearly than by showing what may happen to a child who is deprived of his birthright by having none of the fairy tale element presented to him. In "Father and Son," Mr. Edmund Gosse says:

"Meanwhile, capable as I was of reading, I found my greatest pleasure in the pages of books. The range of these was limited, for storybooks of every description were sternly excluded. No fiction of any kind, religious or secular, was admitted into the house. In this it was to my Mother, not to my Father, that the prohibition was due. She had a remarkable, I confess, to me somewhat unaccountable impression that to 'tell a story,' that is, to compose fictitious narrative of any kind, was a sin. . . . Nor would she read the chivalrous tales in the verse of Sir Walter Scott, obstinately alleging that they were not true. She would read nothing but lyrical and subjective poetry. As a child, however, she had possessed a passion for making-up stories, and so considerable a skill in it, that she was constantly being begged to indulge others with its exercise. . . . 'When I was a very little child,' she says, 'I used to amuse myself and my brothers with inventing stories such as I had read. Having, I suppose, a naturally restless mind and busy imagination, this soon became the chief pleasure of my life. Unfortunately, my brothers were always fond of encouraging this propensity, and I found in Taylor, my maid, a still greater tempter. I had not known there was any harm in it, until Miss Shore, a Calvinistic governess, finding it out, lectured me severely and told me it was wicked. From that time forth, I considered that to invent a story of any kind was a sin. . . . But the longing to do so grew with violence. . . . The simplicity of Truth was not enough for me. I must needs embroider imagination upon it, and the vanity and wickedness which disgraced my heart are more than I am able to express.' This [the author, her son, adds] is surely a very painful instance of the repression of an instinct."

In contrast to the stifling of the imagination, it is good to recall the story of the great Hermite who, having listened to the discussion of the Monday sitting at the Académie des Sciences (Institut de

France) as to the best way to teach the "young idea how to shoot" in the direction of mathematical genius, said: *"Cultivez l'imagination, messieurs. Tout est là. Si vous voulez des mathématiciens, donnez à vos enfants à lire—des Contes de Fées."*

Another important effect of the story is to develop at an early age sympathy for children of other countries where conditions are different from our own.

I have so constantly to deal with the question of confusion between truth and fiction in the minds of children that it might be useful to offer here an example of the way they make the distinction for themselves.

Mrs. Ewing says on this subject:

"If there are young intellects so imperfect as to be incapable of distinguishing between fancy and falsehood, it is most desirable to develop in them the power to do so, but, as a rule, in childhood, we appreciate the distinction with a vivacity which as elders our care-clogged memories fail to recall."

Mr. P. A. Barnett, in his book on the "Commonsense of Education," says, alluding to fairy-tales:

"Children will *act* them but not act *upon* them, and they will not accept the incidents as part of their effectual belief. They will imagine, to be sure, grotesque worlds, full of admirable and interesting personages to whom strange things might have happened. So much the better: this largeness of imagination is one of the possessions that distinguish the better nurtured child from others less fortunate."

The following passage from Stevenson's essay on "Child Play"[1] will furnish an instance of children's aptitude for creating their own dramatic atmosphere:

"When my cousin and I took our porridge of a morning, we had a device to enliven the course of a meal. He ate his with sugar, and explained it to be a country continually buried under snow. I took mine with milk, and explained it to be a country suffering gradual inundation. You can imagine us exchanging bulletins; how here was an island still unsubmerged, here a valley not yet covered with snow; what inventions were made; how his population lived in cabins on perches and traveled on stilts, and how mine was always in boats; how the interest grew furious as the last corner of safe ground was cut off on all sides and grew smaller every moment; and how, in fine, the food was of altogether secondary importance, and might even have been nauseous, so long as we seasoned it with these dreams. But perhaps the most exciting moments I ever had over a meal were in the case of calf's foot jelly. It was hardly possible not to believe—and you may be quite sure, so far from trying, I did all I could to favor the illusion—that some part of it was hollow,

[1] From "Virginibus Puerisque."

and that sooner or later my spoon would lay open the secret tabernacle of that golden rock. There, might some *Red-Beard* await his hour; there might one find the treasures of the Forty Thieves. And so I quarried on slowly, with bated breath, savoring the interest. Believe me, I had little palate left for the jelly; and though I preferred the taste when I took cream with it, I used often to go without because the cream dimmed the transparent fractures."

In his work on "Imagination," Ribot says: "The free initiative of children is always superior to the imitations we pretend to make for them."

The passage from Robert Louis Stevenson becomes more clear from a scientific point of view when taken in connection with one from Karl Groos' book on the "Psychology of Animal Play":

"The child is wholly absorbed in his play, and yet under the ebb and flow of thought and feeling like still water under wind-swept waves, he has the knowledge that it is pretense after all. Behind the sham 'I' that takes part in the game, stands the unchanged 'I' which regards the sham 'I' with quiet superiority."

Queyrat speaks of play as one of the distinct phases of a child's imagination; it is "essentially a metamorphosis of reality, a transformation of places and things."

Now, to return to the point which Mrs. Ewing

makes, namely, that we should develop in normal children the power of distinguishing between truth and falsehood.

I should suggest including two or three stories which would test that power in children, and if they fail to realize the difference between romancing and telling lies, then it is evident that they need special attention and help along this line. I give the titles of two stories of this kind in the collection at the end of the book.[1]

Thus far we have dealt only with the negative results of stories, but there are more important effects, and I am persuaded that if we are careful in our choice of stories, and artistic in our presentation, so that the truth is framed, so to speak, in the memory, we can unconsciously correct evil tendencies in children which they recognize in themselves only when they have already criticized them in the characters of the story. I have sometimes been misunderstood on this point, and, therefore, I should like to make it quite clear. I do *not* mean that stories should take the place entirely of moral or direct teaching, but that on many occasions they could supplement and strengthen moral teaching, because the dramatic appeal to the imagination is quicker than the moral appeal to the conscience. A child will often resist the latter lest it should make him uncomfortable or appeal to his personal sense of re-

[1] See "Long Bow Story;" "John and the Pig."

sponsibility: it is often not in his power to resist the former, because it has taken possession of him before he is aware of it.

As a concrete example, I offer three verses from a poem entitled, "A Ballad for a Boy," written some twelve years ago by W. Cory, an Eton master. The whole poem is to be found in a book of poems known as "Ionica." [1]

The poem describes a fight between two ships, the French ship, *Téméraire,* and the English ship, *Quebec.* The English ship was destroyed by fire; Farmer, the captain, was killed, and the officers taken prisoners:

They dealt with us as brethren, they mourned for Farmer dead,
And as the wounded captives passed each Breton bowed the head.
Then spoke the French lieutenant:
"'Twas the fire that won, not we.
You never struck your flag to *us;*
You'll go to England free." [2]

'Twas the sixth day of October, seventeen hundred seventy-nine,
A year when nations ventured against us to combine,

[1] Published by George Allen & Co.

[2] This is even a higher spirit than that shown in the advice given in the "Agamemnon" (speaking of the victor's attitude after the taking of Troy):

"Yea, let no craving for forbidden gain
Bid conquerors yield before the darts of greed."

Quebec was burned and Farmer slain, by us remembered not;
But thanks be to the French book wherein they're not forgot.

And you, if you've to fight the French, my youngster, bear in mind
Those seamen of King Louis so chivalrous and kind;
Think of the Breton gentlemen who took our lads to Brest,
And treat some rescued Breton as a comrade and a guest.

But in all our stories, in order to produce desired effects we must refrain from holding, as Burroughs says, "a brief for either side," and we must let the people in the story be judged by their deeds and leave the decision of the children free in this matter.[1]

In a review of Ladd's "Psychology" in the *Academy,* we find a passage which refers as much to the story as to the novel:

"The psychological novelist girds up his loins and sets himself to write little essays on each of his characters. If he have the gift of the thing he may analyze motives with a subtlety which is more than their desert, and exhibit simple folk passing through the most dazzling rotations. If he be a novice, he is reduced to mere crude invention—the result in both

[1] It is curious to find that the story of "Puss-in-Boots" in its variants is sometimes presented with a moral, sometimes without. In the Valley of the Ganges it has *none.* In Cashmere it has one moral, in Zanzibar another.

cases is quite beyond the true purpose of Art. Art —when all is said and done—is a suggestion, and it refuses to be explained. Make it obvious, unfold it in detail, and you reduce it to a dead letter."

Again, there is a sentence by Schopenhauer applied to novels which would apply equally well to stories:

"Skill consists in setting the inner life in motion with the smallest possible array of circumstances, for it is this inner life that excites our interest."

In order to produce an encouraging and lasting effect by means of our stories, we should be careful to introduce a certain number from fiction where virtue is rewarded and vice punished, because to appreciate the fact that "virtue is its own reward" it takes a developed and philosophic mind, or a born saint, of whom there will not, I think, be many among normal children: a comforting fact, on the whole, as the normal teacher is apt to confuse them with prigs.

A grande dame visiting an elementary school listened to the telling of an exciting story from fiction, and was impressed by the thrill of delight which passed through the children. But when the story was finished, she said: "But *oh!* what a pity the story was not taken from actual history!"

Now, not only was this comment quite beside the mark, but the lady in question did not realize that pure fiction has one quality which history cannot have. The historian, bound by fact and accuracy, must often let his hero come to grief. The poet (or, in this case we may call him, in the Greek sense, the "maker" of stories) strives to show *ideal* justice.

What encouragement to virtue, except for the abnormal child, can be offered by the stories of good men coming to grief, such as we find in Miltiades, Phocion, Socrates, Severus, Cicero, Cato and Cæsar?

Sir Philip Sydney says in his "Defence of Poesy":

"Only the poet declining to be held by the limitations of the lawyer, the *historian,* the grammarian, the rhetorician, the logician, the physician, the metaphysician is lifted up with the vigor of his own imagination; doth grow in effect into another nature in making things either better than Nature bringeth forth or quite anew, as the Heroes, Demi-gods, Cyclops, Furies and such like, so as he goeth hand-in-hand with Nature, not inclosed in the narrow range of her gifts but freely ranging within the Zodiac of his own art—*her* world is brazen; the poet only delivers a golden one."

The effect of the story need not stop at the negative task of correcting evil tendencies. There is the positive effect of translating the abstract ideal of the story into concrete action.

I was told by Lady Henry Somerset that when the first set of children came down from London for a fortnight's holiday in the country, she was much startled and shocked by the obscenity of the games they played amongst themselves. Being a sound psychologist, Lady Henry wisely refrained from appearing surprised or from attempting any direct method of reproof. "I saw," she said, "that the 'goody' element would have no effect, so I changed the whole atmosphere by reading to them or telling them the most thrilling medieval tales without any commentary. By the end of the fortnight the activities had all changed. The boys were performing astonishing deeds of prowess, and the girls were allowing themselves to be rescued from burning towers and fetid dungeons." Now, if these deeds of chivalry appear somewhat stilted to us, we can at least realize that, having changed the whole atmosphere of the filthy games, it is easier to translate the deeds into something a little more in accordance with the spirit of the age, and boys will more readily wish later on to save their sisters from dangers more sordid and commonplace than fiery towers and dark dungeons, if they have once performed the deeds in which they had to court danger and self-sacrifice for themselves.

And now we come to the question as to how these effects are to be maintained. In what has already been stated as to the danger of introducing the dogmatic and direct appeal into the story, it is evident that the avoidance of this element is the first means of preserving the story in all its artistic force in the memory of the child. We must be careful, as I point out in the chapter on Questions, not to interfere by comment or question with the atmosphere we have made round the story, or else, in the future, that story will become blurred and overlaid with the remembrance, not of the artistic whole, as presented by the teller of the story, but by some unimportant small side issue raised by an irrelevant question or a superfluous comment.

Many people think that the dramatization of the story by the children themselves helps to maintain the effect produced. Personally, I fear there is the same danger as in the immediate reproduction of the story, namely, that the general dramatic effect may be weakened.

If, however, there is to be dramatization (and I do not wish to dogmatize on the subject), I think it should be confined to facts and not fancies, and this is why I realize the futility of the dramatization of fairy tales.

Horace E. Scudder says on this subject:

"Nothing has done more to vulgarize the fairy than its introduction on the stage. The charm of the fairy tale is its divorce from human experience: the charm of the stage is its realization in miniature of human life. If a frog is heard to speak, if a dog is changed before our eyes into a prince by having cold water dashed over it, the charm of the fairy tale has fled, and, in its place, we have the perplexing pleasure of *legerdemain.* Since the real life of a fairy is in the imagination, a wrong is committed when it is dragged from its shadowy hiding-place and made to turn into ashes under the calcium light of the understanding."[1]

I am bound to admit that the teachers have a case when they plead for this reproducing of the story, and there are three arguments they use the validity of which I admit, but which have nevertheless not converted me, because the loss, to my mind, would exceed the gain.

The first argument they put forward is that the reproduction of the story enables the child to enlarge and improve his vocabulary. Now I greatly sympathize with this point of view, but, as I regard the story hour as a very precious and special one, which I think may have a lasting effect on the character of a child, I do not think it important that, during this hour, a child should be called upon to improve his vocabulary at the expense of the dramatic whole, and at the expense of the literary form in which the story has been presented. It would be like using the Bible for parsing or paraphrase or pronunciation. So far, I believe, the line has been drawn here, though there are blasphemers who have laid impious hands on Milton or Shakespeare for this purpose.

[1] From Hans Christian Andersen, in "Childhood in Literature and Art."

There are surely other lessons, as I have already said in dealing with the reproduction of the story quite apart from the dramatization, lessons more utilitarian in character, which can be used for this purpose: the facts of history (I mean the mere facts as compared with the deep truths), and those of geography. Above all, the grammar lessons are those in which the vocabulary can be enlarged and improved. But I am anxious to keep the story hour apart as dedicated to something higher than these excellent but utilitarian considerations.

The second argument used by the teachers is the joy felt by the children in being allowed to dramatize the stories. This, too, appeals very strongly to me, but there is a means of satisfying their desire and yet protecting the dramatic whole, and that is occasionally to allow children to act out their own dramatic inventions; this, to my mind, has great educational significance: it is original and creative work and, apart from the joy of the immediate performance, there is the interesting process of comparison which can be presented to the children, showing them the difference between their elementary attempts and the finished product of the experienced artist. This difference they can be led to recognize by their own powers of observation if the teachers are not in too great a hurry to point it out themselves.

Here is a short original story, quoted by the

French psychologist, Queyrat, in his "Jeux de l'Enfance," written by a child of five:

"One day I went to sea in a life-boat—all at once I saw an enormous whale, and I jumped out of the boat to catch him, but he was so big that I climbed on his back and rode astride, and all the little fishes laughed to see."

Here is a complete and exciting drama, making a wonderful picture and teeming with adventure. We could scarcely offer anything to so small a child for reproduction that would be a greater stimulus to the imagination.

Here is another, offered by Loti, but the age of the child is not given:

"Once upon a time a little girl out in the Colonies cut open a huge melon, and out popped a green beast and stung her, and the little child died."

Loti adds:

"The phrases 'out in the Colonies' and 'a huge melon' were enough to plunge me suddenly into a dream. As by an apparition, I beheld tropical trees, forests alive with marvelous birds. Oh! the simple magic of the words 'the Colonies'! In my childhood they stood for a multitude of distant sun-scorched countries, with their palm-trees, their enormous flowers, their black natives, their wild beasts, their endless possibilities of adventure."

I quote this in full because it shows so clearly the magic force of words to evoke pictures, without any material representation. It is just the opposite effect of the pictures presented to the bodily eye without the splendid educational opportunity for the child to form his own mental image.

I am more and more convinced that the rare power of visualization is accounted for by the lack of mental practice afforded along these lines.

The third argument used by the teachers in favor of the dramatization of the stories is that it is a means of discovering how much the child has really learned from the story. Now this argument makes absolutely no appeal to me.

My experience, in the first place, has taught me that a child very seldom gives out any account of a deep impression made upon him: it is too sacred and personal. But he very soon learns to know what is expected of him, and he keeps a set of stock sentences which he has found out are acceptable to the teacher. How can we possibly gauge the deep effects of a story in this way, or how can a child, by acting out a story, describe the subtle elements which one has tried to introduce? One might as well try to show with a pint measure how the sun and rain have affected a plant, instead of rejoicing in the beauty of the sure, if slow, growth.

Then, again, why are we in such a hurry to find out what effects have been produced by our stories? Does it matter whether we know today or tomorrow how much a child has understood? For my part, so sure do I feel of the effect that I am willing to wait indefinitely. Only, I must make sure that the first presentation is truly dramatic and artistic.

The teachers of general subjects have a much easier and more simple task. Those who teach science, mathematics, even, to a certain extent, history and literature, are able to gauge with a fair amount of accuracy by means of examination what their pupils have learned. The teaching carried on by means of stories can never be gauged in the same manner.

Carlyle has said:

"Of this thing be certain: wouldst thou plant for Eternity, then plant into the deep infinite faculties of man, his Fantasy and Heart. Wouldst thou plant for Year and Day, then plant into his shallow superficial faculties, his self-love and arithmetical understanding, what will grow there." [1]

If we use this marvelous art of story-telling in the way I have tried to show, then the children who have been confided to our care will one day be able to bring to *us* the tribute which Björnson brought to Hans Christian Andersen:

> Wings you gave to my Imagination,
> Me uplifting to the strange and great;
> Gave my heart the poet's revelation,
> Glorifying things of low estate.

---

[1] "Sartor Resartus," Book III, page 218.

THE ART OF THE STORY-TELLER

When my child-soul hungered all-unknowing,
With great truths its need you satisfied:
Now, a world-worn man, to you is owing
That the child in me has never died.

Translated from the Danish by Emilie Poulson.

CHAPTER VII

QUESTIONS ASKED BY TEACHERS

The following questions have been put to me so often by teachers, in my own country and in America, that I have thought it might be useful to give in my book some of the attempts I have made to answer them; and I wish to record here an expression of gratitude to the teachers who have asked these questions at the close of my lectures. It has enabled me to formulate my views on the subject and to clear up, by means of research and thought, the reason for certain things which I had more or less taken for granted. It has also constantly modified my own point of view, and has prevented me from becoming too dogmatic in dealing with other people's methods.

QUESTION I: *Why do I consider it necessary to spend so many years on the art of story-telling, which takes in, after all, such a restricted portion of literature?*

Just in the same way that an actor thinks it worth while to go through so many years' training to fit him for the stage, although dramatic literature is also only one branch of general literature. The region of storyland is the legitimate stage for children. They crave drama as we do, and because there are comparatively few good story-tellers, children do not have their dramatic needs satisfied. What is the result? We either take them to dramatic performances for grown-up people, or we have children's theaters where the pieces, charming as they may be, are of necessity deprived of the essential elements which constitute a drama—or they are shriveled up to suit the capacity of the child. Therefore, it would seem wiser, while the children are quite young, to keep them to the simple presentation of stories, because with their imagination keener at that period, they have the delight of the inner vision and they do not need, as we do, the artificial stimulus provided by the machinery of the stage.

QUESTION II: *What is to be done if a child asks you: "Is the story true?"*

I hope I shall not be considered Utopian in my ideas if I say that it is quite easy, even with small children, to teach them that the seeing of truth is a relative matter which depends on the eyes of the seer. If we were not afraid to tell our children that all through life there are grown-up people who do not see things that others see, their own difficulties would be helped.

In his "Imagination Créatrice," Queyrat says:

"To get down into the recesses of a child's mind, one would have to become even as he is; we are reduced to interpreting that child in the terms of an adult. The children we observe live and grow in a civilized community, and the result of this is that the development of their imagination is rarely free or complete, for as soon as it rises beyond the average level, the rationalistic education of parents and schoolmasters at once endeavors to curb it. It is restrained in its flight by an antagonistic power which treats it as a kind of incipient madness."

It is quite easy to show children that if one keeps things where they belong, they are true with regard to each other, but that if one drags these things out of the shadowy atmosphere of the "make-believe," and forces them into the land of actual facts, the whole thing is out of gear.

To take a concrete example: The arrival of the coach made from a pumpkin and driven by mice is entirely in harmony with the *Cinderella* surroundings, and I have never heard one child raise any question of the difficulty of traveling in such a coach or of the uncertainty of mice in drawing it. But, suggest to the child that this diminutive vehicle could be driven among the cars of Broadway, or amongst the motor omnibuses in the Strand, and you would bring confusion at once into his mind.

Having once grasped this, the children will lose the idea that fairy stories are just for them, and not for their elders, and from this they will go on to see that it is the child-like mind of the poet and seer that continues to appreciate these things; that it is the dull, heavy person whose eyes so soon become dim and unable to see any more the visions which were once his own.

In his essay on "Poetry and Life," Professor Bradley says:

"It is the effect of poetry, not only by expressing emotion but in other ways also, to bring life into the dead mass of our experience, and to make the world significant."

This applies to children as well as to adults. There may come to the child in the story hour, by some stirring poem or dramatic narration, a sudden flash of the possibilities of life which he had not hitherto realized in the even course of school experience.

"Poetry," says Professor Bradley, "is a way of representing truth; but there is in it, as its detractors have always insisted, a certain untruth or illusion. We need not deny this, so long as we remember that the illusion is conscious, that no one wishes to deceive, and that no one is deceived. But it would be better to say that poetry is false to literal fact for the sake of obtaining a higher truth. First, in order to represent the connection between a more significant part of experience and a less significant, poetry, instead of linking them together by a chain which touches one by one the intermediate objects that connect them, leaps from one to the other. It thus falls at once into conflict with common-sense."

Now, the whole of this passage bears as much on the question of the truth embodied in a fairy tale as a poem, and it would be interesting to take some of these tales and try to discover where they are false to actual fact for the sake of a higher truth.

Let us take, for instance, the story of Cinderella: The coach and pumpkins to which I have alluded, and all the magic part of the story, are false to actual facts as we meet them in our everyday life; but is it not a higher truth that *Cinderella* could escape from her chimney corner by thinking of the brightness outside? In this sense we all travel in pumpkin coaches.

Take the story of Psyche, in any one of the many forms it is presented to us in folk-story. The magic transformation of the lover is false to actual fact; but is it not a higher truth that we are often transformed by circumstance, and that love and courage can overcome most difficulties?

Take the story of the Three Bears. It is not in accordance with established fact that bears should extend hospitality to children who invade their territory. Is it not true in a higher sense that fearlessness often lessens or averts danger?

Take the story of Jack and the Bean Stalk. The rapid growth of the bean stalk and the encounter with the giant are false to literal fact; but is it not a higher truth that the spirit of courage and high adventure leads us straight out of the commonplace and often sordid facts of life?

Now, all these considerations are too subtle for the child, and, if offered in explanation, would destroy the excitement and interest of the story; but they are good for those of us who are presenting such stories: they provide not only an argument against the objection raised by unimaginative people as to the futility, if not immorality, of presenting these primitive tales, but clear up our own doubt and justify us in the use of them, if we need such justification.

For myself, I am perfectly satisfied that, being part of the history of primitive people, it would be foolish to ignore them from an evolutionary point of view, which constitutes their chief importance; and it is only from the point of view of expediency that I mention the potential truths they contain.

QUESTION III: *What are you to do if a child says he does not like fairy tales?*

This is not an uncommon case. What we have first to determine, under these circumstances, is whether this dislike springs from a stolid, prosaic nature, whether it springs from a real inability to visualize such pictures as the fairy or marvelous element in the story presents, or whether (and this is often the real reason) it is from a fear of being asked to believe what his judgment resents as untrue, or whether he thinks it is "grown-up" to reject such pleasure as unworthy of his years.

In the first case, it is wise to persevere, in hopes of developing the dormant imagination. If the child resents the apparent want of truth, we can teach him how many-sided truth is, as I suggested in my answer to the first question. In the other cases, we must try to make it clear that the delight he may venture to take now will increase, not decrease, with years; that the more one brings *to* a thing, in the way of experience and knowledge, the more one will draw *out* of it.

Let us take as a concrete example the question of Santa Claus. This joy has almost disappeared, for we have torn away the last shred of mystery about that personage by allowing him to be materialized in the Christmas shops and bazaars.

But the original myth need never have disappeared; the link could easily have been kept by gradually telling the child that the Santa Claus they worshiped as a mysterious and invisible power is nothing but the spirit of charity and kindness that makes us remember others, and that this spirit often takes the form of material gifts. We can also lead them a step higher and show them that this spirit of kindness can do more than provide material things; so that the old nursery tale has laid a beautiful foundation which need never be pulled up: we can build upon it and add to it all through our lives.

Is not *one* of the reasons that children reject fairy tales this, that such very *poor* material is offered them? There is a dreary flatness about all except the very best which revolts the child of literary appreciation and would fail to strike a spark in the more prosaic.

QUESTION IV: *Do I recommend learning a story by heart, or telling it in one's own words?*

This would largely depend on the kind of story. If the style is classic or if the interest of the story is closely connected with the style, as in Andersen, Kipling or Stevenson, then it is better to commit it absolutely to memory. But if this process should take too long (I mean for those who cannot afford the time to specialize), or if it produces a stilted effect, then it is wiser to read the story many times over, let it soak in, taking notes of certain passages which would add to the dramatic interest of the story, and not trouble about the word accuracy of the whole.

For instance, for very young children the story of *Pandora,* as told in "The Wonder-Book," could be shortened so as to leave principally the dramatic dialogue between the two children, which could be easily committed to memory by the narrator and would appeal most directly to the children. Or for older children: in taking a beautiful medieval story such as "Our Lady's Tumbler," retold by Wickstead, the original text could hardly be presented so as to hold an audience; but while giving up a great deal of the elaborate material, we should try to present many of the characteristic passages which seem to sum up the situation. For instance, before his performance, the *Tumbler* cries: "What am I doing? For there is none here so caitiff but who vies with all the rest in serving God after his trade." And after his act of devotion: "Lady, this is a choice performance. I do it for no other but for you; so aid me God, I do not—for you and for your Son. And this I dare avouch and boast, that for me it is no play-work. But I am serving you, and that pays me."

On the other hand, there are some very gifted narrators who can only tell the story in their own words. I consider that both methods are necessary to the all-round story-teller.

QUESTION V: *How do I set about preparing a story?*

Here again the preparation depends a great deal on the kind of story: whether it has to be committed to memory or rearranged to suit a certain age of child, or told entirely in one's own words. But there is one kind of preparation which is the same for any story, that is, living with it for a long time, until one has really obtained the right atmosphere, and then bringing the characters actually to life in this atmosphere, especially in the case of inanimate objects. This is where Hans Christian Andersen reigns supreme. Horace Scudder says of him: "By some transmigration, souls have passed into tin soldiers, balls, tops, money-pigs, coins, shoes and even such attenuated things as darning-needles, and when, informing these apparent dead and stupid bodies, they begin to make manifestations, it is always in perfect consistency with the ordinary conditions of the bodies they occupy, though the several objects become, by the endowment of souls, suddenly expanded in their capacity." [1]

Now, my test of being ready with such stories is whether I have ceased to look upon such objects *as* inanimate. Let us take some of those quoted from Andersen. First, the *Tin Soldier*. To me, since I have lived in the story, he is a real live hero, holding his own with some of the bravest fighting heroes in history or fiction. As for his being merely of tin, I entirely forget it, except when I realize against what odds he fights, or when I stop to admire the wonderful way Andersen carries out his simile of the old tin spoon—the stiffness of the musket, and the tears of tin.

Take the *Top* and the *Ball,* and, except for the delightful way they discuss the respective merits of

[1] From "Childhood in Literature and Art."

cork and mahogany in their ancestors, you would completely forget that they are not real human beings with the live passions and frailties common to youth.

As for the *Beetle*—who ever thinks of him as a mere entomological specimen? Is he not the symbol of the self-satisfied traveler who learns nothing en route but the importance of his own personality? And the *Darning-Needle?* It is impossible to divorce human interest from the ambition of this little piece of steel.

And this same method applied to the preparation of any story shows that one can sometimes rise from the rôle of mere interpreter to that of creator—that is to say, the objects live afresh for you in response to the appeal you make in recognizing their possibilities of vitality.

As a mere practical suggestion, I would advise that, as soon as one has overcome the difficulties of the text (if actually learning by heart, there is nothing but the drudgery of constant repetition), and as one begins to work the story into true dramatic form, always say the words aloud, and many times aloud, before trying them even on one person. More suggestions come to one in the way of effects from hearing the sounds of the words, and more complete mental pictures, in this way than any other—it is a sort of testing period, the results of which may or may not have to be modified when produced in public. In case of committing to memory, I advise word perfection first, not trying dramatic effects before this is reached; but, on the other hand, if you are using your own words, you can think out the effects as you go along—I mean, during the preparation. Gestures, pauses, facial expression often help to fix the choice of words one decides to use, though here again the public performance will often modify the result. I strongly advise that all gestures be studied before the glass, because this most faithfully recording friend, whose sincerity we dare not question, will prevent glaring errors, and also help by the correction of these to more satisfactory results along positive lines. If your gesture does not satisfy you (and practice will make one more and more critical), it is generally because you have not made sufficient allowance for the power of imagination in your audience. Emphasis in gesture is just as inartistic—and therefore ineffective—as emphasis in tone or language.

Before deciding, however, either on the facial expression or gesture, we must consider the chief characters in the story, and study how we can best—*not* present them, but allow them to present themselves, which is a very different thing. The greatest tribute which can be paid to a story-teller, as to an actor, is that his own personality is temporarily forgotten, because he has so completely identified himself with his rôle.

When we have decided what the chief characters really mean to do, we can let ourselves go in the impersonation.

I shall now take a story as a concrete example. namely, the Buddhist legend of the "Lion and the Hare." [1]

We have here the *Lion* and the *Hare* as types—the other animals are less individual and therefore display less salient qualities. The little hare's chief characteristics are nervousness, fussiness and misdirected imagination. We must bear this all in mind when she appears on the stage—fortunately these characteristics lend themselves easily to dramatic representation. The *Lion* is not only large-hearted but broad-minded. It is good to have an opportunity of presenting to the children a lion who has other qualities than physical beauty or extraordinary strength (here again there will lurk the danger of alarming the nature students). He is even more interesting than the magnanimous lion whom we have sometimes been privileged to meet in fiction.

Of course we grown-up people know that the *Lion* is the Buddha in disguise. Children will not be able to realize this, nor is it the least necessary that they should do so; but they will grasp the idea that he is a very unusual lion, not to be met with in Paul Du Chaillu's adventures, still less in the quasi-domestic atmosphere of the Zoological Gardens. If

---

[1] See "Eastern Stories and Fables," published by Routledge.

our presentation is life-like and sincere, we shall convey all we intend to the child. This is part of what I call the atmosphere of the story, which, as in a photograph, can only be obtained by long exposure, that is to say, in the case of preparation we must bestow much reflection and sympathy.

Because these two animals are the chief characters, they must stand out in sharp outline: the other animals must be painted in fainter colors—they should be suggested rather than presented in detail. It might be as well to give a definite gesture to the *Elephant*—say, a characteristic movement with his trunk—a scowl to the *Tiger,* a supercilious and enigmatic smile to the *Camel* (suggested by Kipling's wonderful creation). But if a gesture were given to each of the animals, the effect would become monotonous, and the minor characters would crowd the foreground of the picture, impeding the action and leaving little to the imagination of the audience. I personally have found it effective to repeat the gestures of these animals as they are leaving the stage, but less markedly, as it is only a form of reminder.

Now, what is the impression we wish to leave on the mind of the child, apart from the dramatic joy and interest we have endeavored to provide? Surely it is that he may realize the danger of a panic. One method of doing this (alas! a favorite one still) is to say at the end of the story: "Now, children, what do we learn from this?" Of this method Lord Morley has said: "It is a commonplace to the wise, and an everlasting puzzle to the foolish, that direct inculcation of morals should invariably prove so powerless an instrument, so futile a method."

If this direct method were really effective, we might as well put the little drama aside, and say plainly: "It is foolish to be nervous; it is dangerous to make loose statements. Large-minded people understand things better than those who are narrow-minded."

All these abstract statements would be as true and as tiresome as the multiplication table. The child might or might not fix them in his mind, but he would not act upon them.

But, put all the artistic warmth of which you are capable into the presentation of the story, and, without one word of comment from you, the children will feel the dramatic intensity of that vast concourse of animals brought together by the feeble utterance of one irresponsible little hare. Let them feel the dignity and calm of the *Lion,* which accounts for his authority; his tender but firm treatment of the foolish little *Hare;* and listen to the glorious finale when all the animals retire convinced of their folly; and you will find that you have adopted the same method as the *Lion* (who must have been an unconscious follower of Froebel), and that there is nothing to add to the picture.

QUESTION VI: *Is it wise to talk over a story with children and to encourage them in the habit of asking questions about it?*

At the time, no! The effect produced is to be by dramatic means, and this would be destroyed by any attempt at analysis by means of questions.

The medium that has been used in the telling of the story is (or ought to be) a purely artistic one which will reach the child through the medium of the emotions: the appeal to the intellect or the reason is a different method, which must be used at a different time. When you are enjoying the fragrance of a flower or the beauty of its color, it is not the moment to be reminded of its botanical classification, just as in the botany lesson it would be somewhat irrelevant to talk of the part that flowers play in the happiness of life.

From a practical point of view, it is not wise to encourage questions on the part of the children, because they are apt to disturb the atmosphere by bringing in entirely irrelevant matter, so that in looking back on the telling of the story, the child often remembers the irrelevant conversation to the exclusion of the dramatic interest of the story itself.[1]

I remember once making what I considered at the time a most effective appeal to some children who

[1] See Chapter I.

had been listening to the Story of the Little Tin Soldier, and, unable to refrain from the cheap method of questioning, of which I have now recognized the futility, I asked: "Don't you think it was nice of the little dancer to rush down into the fire to join the brave little soldier?" "Well," said a prosaic little lad of six. "I thought the draught carried her down."

QUESTION VII: *Is it wise to call upon children to repeat the story as soon as it has been told?*

My answer here is decidedly in the negative.

While fully appreciating the modern idea of children expressing themselves, I very much deprecate this so-called self-expression taking the form of mere reproduction. I have dealt with this matter in detail in another portion of my book. This is one of the occasions when children should be taking in, not giving out (even the most fanatic of moderns must agree that there *are* such moments).

When, after much careful preparation, an expert has told a story to the best of his ability, to encourage the children to reproduce this story with their imperfect vocabulary and with no special gift of speech (I am always alluding to the normal group of children) is as futile as if, after the performance of a musical piece by a great artist, some individual member of the audience were to be called upon to give *his* rendering of the original rendering. The result would be that the musical joy of the audience would be completely destroyed and the performer himself would share in the loss.[1]

I have always maintained that five minutes of complete silence after the story would do more to fix the impression on the mind of the child than any amount of attempt at reproducing it. The general statement made in Dr. Montessori's wonderful chapter on "Silence" would seem to me of special application to the moments following on the telling of a story.

QUESTION VIII: *Should children be encouraged to illustrate the stories which they have heard?*

As a dramatic interest to the teachers and the children, I think it is a very praiseworthy experiment, if used somewhat sparingly. But I seriously doubt whether these illustrations in any way indicate the impression made on the mind of the child. It is the same question that arises when that child is called upon, or expresses a wish, to reproduce the story in his own words: the unfamiliar medium in both instances makes it almost impossible for the child to convey his meaning, unless he is an artist in the one case or he has real literary power of expression in the other.

[1] In this matter I have, in England, the support of Dr. Kimmins, Chief Inspector of Education in the London County Council, who is strongly opposed to the immediate reproduction of stories.

My own impression, confirmed by many teachers who have made the experiment, is that a certain amount of disappointment is mixed up with the daring joy in the attempt, simply because the children can get nowhere near the ideal which has presented itself to the "inner eye."

I remember a kindergarten teacher saying that on one occasion, when she had told to the class a thrilling story of a knight, one of the children immediately asked for permission to draw a picture of him on the blackboard. So spontaneous a request could not, of course, be refused, and, full of assurance, the would-be artist began to give his impression of the knight's appearance. When the picture was finished, the child stood back for a moment to judge for himself of the result. He put down the chalk and said sadly: "And I *thought* he was so handsome."

Nevertheless, except for the drawback of the other children seeing a picture which might be inferior to their own mental vision, I should quite approve of such experiments, as long as they are not taken as literal data of what the children have really received. It would, however, be better not to have the picture drawn on a blackboard but at the child's private desk, to be seen by the teacher and not, unless the picture were exceptionally good, to be shown to the other children.

One of the best effects of such an experiment

would be to show a child how difficult it is to give the impression one wishes to record, and which would enable him later on to appreciate the beauty of such work in the hands of a finished artist.

I can anticipate the jeers with which such remarks would be received by the Futurist School, but, according to their own theory, I ought to be allowed to express the matter *as I see it,* however faulty the vision may appear to them.[1]

QUESTION IX: *In what way can the dramatic method of story-telling be used in ordinary class teaching?*

This is too large a question to answer fully in so general a survey as this work, but I should like to give one or two examples as to how the element of story-telling could be introduced.

I have always thought that the only way in which we could make either a history or literature lesson live, so as to take a real hold on the mind of the pupil at any age, would be that, instead of offering lists of events, crowded into the fictitious area of one reign, one should take a single event, say in one lesson out of five, and give it in the most splendid language and in the most dramatic manner.

---

[1] These remarks refer only to the illustrations of stories told. Whether children should be encouraged to self-expression in drawing (quite apart from reproducing in one medium what has been conveyed to them in another), is too large a question to deal with in this special work on story-telling.

To come to a concrete example: Supposing that one is talking to the class of Greece, either in connection with its history, its geography or its literature, could any mere accumulation of facts give a clearer idea of the life of the people than a dramatically told story from Homer, Æschylus, Sophocles or Euripides?

What in the history of Iceland could give any more graphic idea of the whole character of the life and customs of the inhabitants than one of the famous sagas, such as "The Burning of Njal" or "The Death of Gunnar"?

In teaching the history of Spain, what could make the pupils understand better the spirit of knight-errantry, its faults and its qualities, than a recital from "Don Quixote" or from the tale of "The Cid"?

In a word, the stories must appeal so vividly to the imagination that they will light up the whole period of history which we wish them to illustrate and keep it alive in the memory for all time.

But quite apart from the dramatic presentation of history, there are very great possibilities for the short story introduced into the portrait of some great personage, insignificant in itself, but which throws a sudden sidelight on his character, showing the mind behind the actual deeds; this is what I mean by using the dramatic method.

To take a concrete example: Suppose, in giving

an account of the life of Napoleon, after enlarging upon his campaigns, his European policy, his indomitable will, one were suddenly to give an idea of his many-sidedness by relating how he actually found time to compile a catechism which was used for some years in the elementary schools of France. What sidelights might be thrown in this way on such characters as Nero, Cæsar, Henry VIII, Luther, Goethe!

To take one example from these: Instead of making the whole career of Henry VIII center round the fact that he was a much-married man, could we not present his artistic side and speak of his charming contributions to music?

So much for the history lessons. But could not the dramatic form and interest be introduced into our geography lessons? Think of the romance of the Panama Canal, the position of Constantinople, as affecting the history of Europe, the shape of Greece, England as an island, the position of Thibet, the interior of Africa—to what wonderful story-telling would these themes lend themselves!

QUESTION X: *Which should predominate in the story—the dramatic or the poetic element?*

This is a much debated point. From experience I have come to the conclusion that, though both should be found in the whole range of stories, the dramatic element should prevail from the very nature of the presentation, and also because it reaches the larger number of children, at least of normal children. Almost every child is dramatic, in the sense that it loves action (not necessarily an action in which it has to bear a part). It is the exceptional child who is reached by the poetic side, and just as on the stage the action must be quicker and more concentrated than in a poem—than even a dramatic poem—so it must be with the story. Children act out in their imagination the dramatic or actable part of the story—the poetical side, which must be painted in more delicate colors or presented in less obvious form, often escapes them. Of course, the very reason why we must include the poetical element is that it is an unexpressed need of most children. Their need of the dramatic is more loudly proclaimed and more easily satisfied.

QUESTION XI: *What is the educational value of humor in the stories told to our children?*

My answer to this is that humor means so much more than is usually understood by this term. So many people seem to think that to have a sense of humor is merely to be tickled by a funny element in a story. It surely means something much more subtle than this. It is Thackeray who says: "If humor only meant laughter, but the humorist professes to awaken and direct your love, your pity, your kindness, your scorn for untruth and pretension, your tenderness for the weak, the poor, the oppressed, the unhappy." So that, in our stories, the introduction of humor should not merely depend on the doubtful amusement that follows on a sense of incongruity. It should inculcate a sense of proportion brought about by an effort of imagination; it shows a child its real position in the universe and prevents an exaggerated idea of his own importance. It develops the logical faculty, and prevents hasty conclusions. It shortens the period of joy in horse-play and practical jokes. It brings about a clearer perception of all situations, enabling the child to get the point of view of another person. It is the first instilling of philosophy into the mind of a child and prevents much suffering later on when the blows of life fall upon him; for a sense of humor teaches us at an early age not to expect too much: and this philosophy can be developed without cynicism or pessimism, without even destroying the *joie de vivre*.

One cannot, however, sufficiently emphasize the fact that these far-reaching results can be brought about only by humor quite distinct from the broader fun and hilarity which have also their use in an educational scheme.

From my own experience, I have learned that development of humor is with most children extremely slow. It *is* quite natural and quite right that at first pure fun, obvious situations and elementary jokes should please them, but we can very gradually appeal to something more subtle, and if I were asked what story would educate our children most thoroughly in appreciation of humor, I should say that "Alice in Wonderland" was the most effective.

What better object lesson could be given in humorous form of taking somebody else's point of view than that given to *Alice* by the *Mock Turtle* in speaking of the *Whiting?*—

> "You know what they're like?"
> "I believe so," said Alice. "They have their tails in their mouths—and they're all over crumbs."
> "You're wrong about the crumbs," said the Mock Turtle. "Crumbs would all wash off in the sea."

Or when *Alice* is speaking to the *Mouse* of her cat, and says:

> "She is such a dear quiet thing—and a capital one for catching mice——" and then suddenly realizes the point of view of the *Mouse,* who was "trembling down to the end of its tail."

Then, as an instance of how a lack of humor leads to illogical conclusons (a condition common to most children), we have the conversation between *Alice* and the *Pigeon:*

> ALICE: "But little girls eat quite as much as serpents do, you know."
> PIGEON: "I don't believe it. But if they do, why then they're a kind of serpent, that's all I can say."

Then, as an instance of how a sense of humor would prevent too much self-importance:

"I have a right to think," said Alice sharply.

"Just about as much right," said the Duchess, "as pigs have to fly."

PART II

THE STORIES

The following stories do not form a comprehensive selection. The stories given are chiefly taken from my own repertoire, and have been so constantly asked for by teachers that I am glad of an opportunity of presenting them in full.

I regret that I have been unable to furnish many of the stories I consider good for narration, but the difficulty of obtaining permission has deterred me from further efforts in this direction.

STURLA, THE HISTORIAN[1]

Then Sturla got ready to sail away with the king, and his name was put on the list. He went on board before many men had come; he had a sleeping bag and a travelling chest, and took his place on the foredeck. A little later the king came on to the quay, and a company of men with him. Sturla rose and bowed, and bade the king "hail," but the king answered nothing, and went aft along the ship to the quarter-deck. They sailed that day to go south along the coast. But in the evening when men unpacked their provisions Sturla sat still, and no one invited him to mess. Then a servant of the king's came and asked Sturla if he had any meat and drink. Sturla said "No." Then the king's servant went to the king and spoke with him, out of hearing, and then went forward to Sturla and said: "You shall go to mess with Thorir Mouth and Erlend Maw." They took him into their mess, but rather stiffly. When men were turning in to sleep, a sailor of the king's asked who should tell them stories. There

---

[1] I give the following story, quoted by Professor Ker in his Romanes lecture, 1906, as an encouragement to those who develop the art of story-telling.

was little answer. Then said he: "Sturla the Icelander, will you tell stories?" "As you will," said Sturla. So he told them the story of Huld, better and fuller than any one there had ever heard it told before. Then many men pushed forward to the fore-deck, wanting to hear as clearly as might be, and there was a great crowd. The queen asked: "What is that crowd on deck there?" A man answered: "The men are listening to the story that the Icelander tells." "What story is that?" said she. He answers: "It is about a great troll-wife, and it is a good story and well told." The king bade her pay no heed to that, and go to sleep. She says: "I think this Icelander must be a good fellow, and less to blame than he is reported." The king was silent.

So the night passed, and the next morning there was no wind for them, and the king's ship lay in the same place. Later in the day, when men sat at their drink, the king sent dishes from his table to Sturla. Sturla's messmates were pleased with this: "You bring better luck than we thought, if this sort of thing goes on." After dinner the queen sent for Sturla and asked him to come to her and bring the troll-wife story along with him. So Sturla went aft to the quarter-deck, and greeted the king and queen. The king answered little, the queen well and cheerfully. She asked him to tell the same story he had told overnight. He did so, for a great part of the day. When he had finished, the queen thanked him, and many others besides, and made him out in their minds to be a learned man and sensible. But the king said nothing; only he smiled a little. Sturla thought he saw that the king's whole frame of mind was brighter than the day before. So he said to the king that he had made a poem about him, and another about his father: "I would gladly get a hearing for them." The queen said: "Let him recite his poem; I am told that he is the best of poets, and his poem will be excellent." The king bade him say on, if he would, and repeat the poem he professed to have made about him. Sturla chanted it to the end. The queen said: "To my mind that is a good poem." The king said to her: "Can you follow the poem clearly?" "I would be fain to have you think so, Sir," said the queen. The king said: "I have learned that Sturla is good at verses." Sturla took his leave of the king and queen and went to his place. There was no sailing for the king all that day. In the evening before he went to bed he sent for Sturla. And when he came he greeted the king and said: "What will you have me to do, Sir?" The king called for a silver goblet full of wine, and drank some and gave it to Sturla and said: "A health to a friend in wine!" (*Vin skal til vinar drekka*). Sturla said: "God be praised for it!" "Even so," says the king, "and now I wish you to say the poem you have made about my father." Sturla repeated it: and when it was finished men praised it much, and most of all the queen. The king said: "To my thinking, you are a better reciter than the Pope."

Sturlunga Saga, vol. ii, p. 269.

A SAGA

In the grey beginnings of the world, or ever the flower of justice had rooted in the heart, there lived among the daughters of men two children, sisters, of one house.

In childhood did they leap and climb and swim with the men children of their race, and were nurtured on the same stories of gods and heroes.

In maidenhood they could do all that a maiden might and more—delve could they no less than spin, hunt no less than weave, brew pottage and helm ships, wake the harp and tell the stars, face all danger and laugh at all pain.

Joyous in toil-time and rest-time were they as the days and years of their youth came and went. Death had spared their house, and unhappiness knew they none. Yet often as at falling day they sat before sleep round the hearth of red fire, listening with the household to the brave songs of gods and heroes, there would surely creep into their hearts a shadow—the thought that whatever the years of their lives, and whatever the generous deeds, there would for them, as women, be no escape at the last from the dire mists of Hela, the fogland beyond the grave for all such as die not in battle; no escape for them from Hela, and no place for ever for them or for their kind among the glory-crowned, sword-shriven heroes of echoing Valhalla.

That shadow had first fallen in their lusty childhood, had slowly gathered darkness through the overflowing days of maidenhood, and now, in the strong tide of full womanhood, often lay upon their future as the moon in Odin's wrath lies upon the sun.

But stout were they to face danger and laugh at pain, and for all the shadow upon their hope they lived brave and songful days—the one a homekeeper and in her turn a mother of men; the other unhusbanded, but gentle to ignorance and sickness and sorrow through the width and length of the land.

And thus, facing life fearlessly and ever with a smile, those two women lived even unto extreme old age, unto the one's children's children's children, labouring truly unto the end and keeping strong hearts against the dread day of Hela, and the fate-locked gates of Valhalla.

But at the end a wonder.

As these sisters looked their last upon the sun, the one in the ancestral homestead under the eyes of love, the other in a distant land among strange faces, behold the wind of Thor, and out of the deep of heaven the white horses of Odin, All-Father, bearing Valkyrie, shining messengers of Valhalla. And those two world-worn women, faithful in all their lives, were caught up in death in divine arms and borne far from the fogs of Hela to golden thrones among the battle heroes, upon which the Nornir, sitting at the loom of life, had from all eternity graven their names.

And from that hour have the gates of Valhalla been thrown wide to all faithful endeavour whether of man or of woman.

By John Russell, Headmaster of the King Alfred School.

THE LEGEND OF ST. CHRISTOPHER

Christopher was of the lineage of the Canaaneans and he was of a right great stature, and had a terrible and fearful cheer and countenance. And he was twelve cubits of length. And, as it is read in some histories, when he served and dwelled with the king of Canaaneans, it came in his mind that he would seek the greatest prince that was in the world and him he would serve and obey.

And so far he went that he came to a right great king, of whom the renown generally was that he was the greatest of the world. And when the king saw him he received him into his service and made him to dwell in his court.

Upon a time a minstrel sung tofore him a song in which he named oft the devil. And the king which was a Christian man, when he heard him name the devil, made anon the sign of the cross in his visage. And when Christopher saw that, he had great marvel what sign it was and wherefore the king made it. And he demanded it of him. And because the king would not say, he said, "If thou tell me not, I shall no longer dwell with thee." And then the king told to him saying, "Alway when I hear the devil named, I fear that he should have power over me, and I garnish me with this sign that he grieve not nor annoy me." Then Christopher said to him, "Thou doubtest the devil that he hurt thee not? Then is the devil more mighty and greater than thou art. I am then deceived of my hope and purpose; for I supposed that I had found the most mighty and the most greatest lord of the world. But I commend thee to God, for I will go seek him to be my lord and I his servant."

And then he departed from this king and hasted him to seek the devil. And as he went by a great desert he saw a great company of knights. Of which a knight cruel and horrible came to him and demanded whither he went. And Christopher answered to him and said, "I go to seek the devil for to be my master." And he said, "I am he that thou seekest." And then Christopher was glad and bound himself to be his servant perpetual, and took him for his master and lord.

And as they went together by a common way, they found there a cross erect and standing. And anon as the devil saw the cross, he was afeard and fled, and left the right way and brought Christopher about by a sharp desert, and after, when they were past the cross, he brought him to the highway that they had left. And when Christopher saw that, he marvelled and demanded whereof he doubted that he had left high and fair way and had gone so far about by so hard desert. And the devil would not tell to him in no wise. Then Christopher said to him, "If thou wilt not tell me I shall anon depart from thee and shall serve thee no more." Therefore the devil was constrained to tell him, and said, "There was a man called Christ which was hanged on the cross, and when I see his sign, I am sore afeard and flee from it wheresomever I find it." To whom Christopher said, "Then he is greater and more mightier than thou, when thou art afraid of his sign. And I see well that I have laboured in vain since I have not founden the greatest lord of all the earth. And I will serve thee no longer. Go thy way then: for I will go seek Jesus Christ."

And when he had long sought and demanded where he should find Christ, at the last he came into a great desert to an hermit that dwelled there. And this hermit preached to him of Jesus Christ and informed him in the faith diligently. And he said to him, "This king whom thou desirest to serve, requireth this service that thou must oft fast." And Christopher said to him, "Require of me some other thing and I shall do it. For that which thou requirest I may not do." And the hermit said, "Thou must then wake and make many prayers." And Christopher said to him, "I wot not what it is. I may do no such thing." And then the hermit said unto him, "Knowest thou such a river in which many be perished and lost?" To whom Christopher said, "I know it well." Then said the hermit, "Because thou art noble and high of stature and strong in thy members, thou shalt be resident by that river and shalt bear over all them that shall pass there. Which shall be a thing right convenable to Our Lord Jesus Christ, whom thou desirest to serve, and I hope He shall show Himself to thee." Then said Christopher, "Certes, this service may I well do, and I promise to Him for to do it."

Then went Christopher to this river, and made there his habitation for him. And he bare a great pole in his hand instead of a staff, by which he sustained him in the water; and bare over all manner of people without ceasing. And there he abode, thus doing, many days.

And on a time, as he slept in his lodge, he heard the voice of a child which called him and said, "Christopher, come out and bear me over." Then he awoke and went out; but he found no man. And when he was again in his house, he heard the same voice, and he ran out and found no body. The third time he was called, and came thither, and found a child beside the rivage of the river: which prayed him goodly to bear him over the water. And then Christopher lift up the child on his shoulders and took his staff and entered in to the river for to pass. And the water of the river arose and swelled more and more. And the child was heavy as lead. And always as he went further the water increased and grew more, and the child more and more waxed heavy: in so much that Christopher had great anguish and feared to be drowned. And when he was escaped with great pain and passed the water, and set the child aground, he said to the child, "Child, thou hast put me in great peril. Thou weighest almost as I had had all the world upon me. I might bear no greater burden." And the child answered, "Christopher, marvel thou no thing. For thou hast not only borne all the world upon thee; but thou hast borne Him that created and made all the world upon thy shoulders. I am Jesus Christ, the king to whom thou servest in this work. And that thou mayest know that I say to thee truth, set thy staff in the earth by the house, and thou shalt see to-morrow that it shall bear flowers and fruit." And anon he vanished from his eyes.

And then Christopher set his staff in the earth and when he arose on the morrow, he found his staff like a palm-tree bearing flowers, leaves and dates.

From *The Legenda Aurea* (Temple Classics).

ARTHUR IN THE CAVE

Once upon a time a Welshman was walking on London Bridge, staring at the traffic and wondering why there were so many kites hovering about. He had come to London, after many adventures with thieves and highwaymen, which need not be related here, in charge of a herd of black Welsh cattle. He had sold them with much profit, and with jingling gold in his pocket he was going about to see the sights of the city.

He was carrying a hazel staff in his hand, for you must know that a good staff is as necessary to a drover as teeth are to his dogs. He stood still to gaze at some wares in a shop (for at that time London Bridge was shops from beginning to end), when he noticed that a man was looking at his stick with a long fixed look. The man after a while came to him and asked him where he came from.

"I come from my own country," said the Welshman, rather surlily, for he could not see what business the man had to ask such a question.

"Do not take it amiss," said the stranger: "if you will only answer my questions, and take my advice, it will be of greater benefit to you than you imagine. Do you remember where you cut that stick?"

The Welshman was still suspicious, and said: "What does it matter where I cut it?"

"It matters," said the questioner, "because there is a treasure hidden near the spot where you cut that stick. If you can remember the place and conduct me to it, I will put you in possession of great riches."

The Welshman now understood he had to deal with a sorcerer, and he was greatly perplexed as to what to do. On the one hand, he was tempted by the prospect of wealth; on the other hand, he knew that the sorcerer must have derived his knowledge from devils, and he feared to have anything to do with the powers of darkness. The cunning man strove hard to persuade him, and at length made him promise to shew the place where he cut his hazel staff.

The Welshman and the magician journeyed together to Wales. They went to Craig y Dinas, the Rock of the Fortress, at the head of the Neath valley, near Pont Nedd Fechan, and the Welshman, pointing to the stock or root of an old hazel, said: "This is where I cut my stick."

"Let us dig," said the sorcerer. They digged until they came to a broad, flat stone. Prying this up, they found some steps leading downwards. They went down the steps and along a narrow passage until they came to a door. "Are you brave?" asked the sorcerer; "will you come in with me?"

"I will," said the Welshman, his curiosity getting the better of his fear.

They opened the door, and a great cave opened out before them. There was a faint red light in the cave, and they could see everything. The first thing they came to was a bell.

"Do not touch that bell," said the sorcerer, "or it will be all over with us both."

As they went further in, the Welshman saw that the place was not empty. There were soldiers lying down asleep, thousands of them, as far as ever the eye could see. Each one was clad in bright armour, the steel helmet of each was on his head, the shining shield of each was on his arm, the sword of each was near his hand, each had his spear stuck in the ground near him, and each and all were asleep.

In the midst of the cave was a great round table at which sat warriors whose noble features and richly-dight armour proclaimed that they were not as the roll of common men.

Each of these, too, had his head bent down in sleep. On a golden throne on the further side of the round table was a king of gigantic stature and august presence. In his hand, held below the hilt, was a mighty sword with scabbard and haft of gold studded with gleaming gems; on his head was a crown set with precious stones which flashed and glinted like so many points of fire. Sleep had set its seal on his eyelids also.

"Are they asleep?" asked the Welshman, hardly believing his own eyes. "Yes, each and all of them," answered the sorcerer. "But, if you touch yonder bell, they will all awake."

"How long have they been asleep?"

"For over a thousand years."

"Who are they?"

"Arthur's warriors, waiting for the time to come when they shall destroy all the enemy of the Cymry and re-possess the strand of Britain, establishing their own king once more at Caer Lleon."

"Who are these sitting at the round table?"

"These are Arthur's knights—Owain, the son of Urien; Cai, the son of Cynyr; Gnalchmai, the son of Gwyar; Peredir, the son of Efrawe; Geraint, the son of Erbin; Trystan, the son of March; Bedwyr, the son of Bedrawd; Ciernay, the son of Celyddon; Edeyrn, the son of Nudd; Cymri, the son of Clydno."

"And on the golden throne?" broke in the Welshman.

"Is Arthur himself, with his sword Excalibur in his hand," replied the sorcerer.

Impatient by this time at the Welshman's questions, the sorcerer hastened to a great heap of yellow gold on the floor of the cave. He took up as much as he could carry, and bade his companion do the same. "It is time for us to go," he then said, and he led the way towards the door by which they had entered.

But the Welshman was fascinated by the sight of the countless soldiers in their glittering arms—all asleep.

"How I should like to see them all awaking!" he said to himself. "I will touch the bell—I *must* see them all arising from their sleep."

When they came to the bell, he struck it until it rang through the whole place. As soon as it rang, lo! the thousands of warriors leapt to their feet and the ground beneath them shook with the sound of the steel arms. And a great voice came from their midst: "Who rang the bell? Has the day come?"

The sorcerer was so much frightened that he shook like an aspen leaf. He shouted in answer: "No, the day has not come. Sleep on."

The mighty host was all in motion, and the Welshman's eyes were dazzled as he looked at the bright steel arms which illumined the cave as with the light of myriad flames of fire.

"Arthur," said the voice again, "awake; the bell has rung, the day is breaking. Awake, Arthur the Great."

"No," shouted the sorcerer, "it is still night. Sleep on, Arthur the Great."

A sound came from the throne. Arthur was standing, and the jewels in his crown shone like bright stars above the countless throng. His voice was strong and sweet like the sound of many waters, and he said:

"My warriors, the day has not come when the Black Eagle and the Golden Eagle shall go to war. It is only a seeker after gold who has rung the bell. Sleep on, my warriors; the morn of Wales has not yet dawned."

A peaceful sound like the distant sigh of the sea came over the cave, and in a trice the soldiers were all asleep again. The sorcerer hurried the Welshman out of the cave, moved the stone back to its place and vanished.

Many a time did the Welshman try to find his way into the cave again, but though he dug over every inch of the hill, he has never again found the entrance to Arthur's Cave.

From *The Welsh Fairy Book,* by W. Jenkyn Thomas (Fisher Unwin).

HAFIZ, THE STONE-CUTTER

There was once a stone-cutter whose name was Hafiz, and all day long he chipped, chipped, chipped at his block. And often he grew very weary of his task and he would say to himself impatiently, "Why should I go on chip-chip-chipping at my block? Why should I not have pleasure and amusement as other folk have?"

One day, when the sun was very hot and when he felt specially weary, he suddenly heard the sound of many feet, and, looking up from his work, he saw a great procession coming his way. It was the King, mounted on a splendid charger, all his soldiers to the right, in their shining armour, and the servants to the left, dressed in gorgeous clothing, ready to do his behests.

And Hafiz said: "How splendid to be a King! If only I could be a King, if only for ten minutes, so that I might know what it feels like!" And then, even as he spoke, he seemed to be dreaming, and in his dream he sang this little song:

> "Ah me! Ah me!
> If Hafiz only the King could be!" [1]

[1] The melody to be crooned at first and to grow louder at each incident.

And then a voice from the air around seemed to answer him and to say:

"Be thou the King."

And Hafiz became the King, and he it was that sat on the splendid charger, and they were his soldiers to the right and his servants to the left. And Hafiz said: "I am King, and there is no one stronger in the whole world than I."

But soon, in spite of the golden canopy over his head, Hafiz began to feel the terrible heat of the rays of the sun, and soon he noticed that the soldiers and servants were weary, that his horse drooped, and that he, Hafiz, was overcome, and he said angrily: "What! Is there something stronger in the world than a King?" And, almost without knowing it, he again sang his song—more boldly than the first time:

"Ah me! Ah me!
If Hafiz only the Sun could be!"

And the Voice answered:

"Be thou the Sun."

And Hafiz became the Sun, and shone down upon the Earth, but, because he did not know how to shine very wisely, he shone very fiercely, so that the crops dried up, and folk grew sick and died. And then there arose from the East a little cloud which slipped between Hafiz and the Earth, so that he could no longer shine down upon it, and he said: "Is there something stronger in the world than the Sun?"

"Ah me! Ah me!
If Hafiz only the Cloud could be!"

And the Voice said:

"Be thou the Cloud."

And Hafiz became the Cloud, and rained down water upon the Earth, but, because he did not know how to do so wisely, there fell so much rain that all the little rivulets became great rivers, and all the great rivers overflowed their banks, and carried everything before them in swift torrent—all except one great rock which stood unmoved. And Hafiz said: "Is there something stronger than the Cloud?

"Ah me! Ah me!
If Hafiz only the Rock could be!"

And the Voice said:

"Be thou the Rock."

And Hafiz became the Rock, and the Cloud disappeared and the waters went down.

And Hafiz the Rock saw coming towards him a man—but he could not see his face. As the man approached he suddenly raised a hammer and struck

Hafiz, so that he felt it through all his stony body. And Hafiz said: "Is there something stronger in the world than the Rock?

"Ah me! Ah me!
If Hafiz only that Man might be!"

And the Voice said:

"Be thou—Thyself."

And Hafiz seized the hammer and said:

"The Sun was stronger than the King, the Cloud was stronger than the Sun, the Rock was stronger than the Cloud, but I, Hafiz, was stronger than all."

Adapted and arranged by M. L. Shedlock.

TO YOUR GOOD HEALTH

(*From the Russian*)

Long long ago there lived a King who was such a mighty monarch that whenever he sneezed everyone in the whole country had to say, "To your good health!" Everyone said it except the Shepherd with the bright blue eyes, and he would not say it.

The King heard of this and was very angry, and sent for the Shepherd to appear before him.

The Shepherd came and stood before the throne, where the King sat looking very grand and powerful. But however grand or powerful he might be, the Shepherd did not feel a bit afraid of him.

"Say at once 'To my good health!' cried the King.

"To my good health," replied the Shepherd.

"To mine—to *mine,* you rascal, you vagabond!" stormed the King.

"To mine, to mine, Your Majesty," was the answer.

"But to *mine*—to my own!" roared the King, and beat on his breast in a rage.

"Well, yes; to mine, of course, to my own," cried the Shepherd, and gently tapped his breast.

The King was beside himself with fury and did not know what to do, when the Lord Chamberlain interfered:

"Say at once—say this very moment, 'To your health, Your Majesty,' for if you don't say it you will lose your life," he whispered.

"No, I won't say it till I get the Princess for my wife," was the Shepherd's answer.

Now the Princess was sitting on a little throne beside the King, her father, and she looked as sweet and lovely as a little golden dove. When she heard what the Shepherd said, she could not help laughing, for there is no denying the fact that this young shepherd with the blue eyes pleased her very much; indeed, he pleased her better than any king's son she had yet seen.

But the King was not as pleasant as his daughter, and he gave orders to throw the Shepherd into the white bear's pit.

The guards led him away and thrust him into the pit with the white bear, who had had nothing to eat for two days and was very hungry. The door of the pit was hardly closed when the bear rushed at the Shepherd; but when it saw his eyes it was so frightened that it was ready to eat itself. It shrank away into a corner and gazed at him from there, and in spite of being so famished, did not dare to touch him, but sucked its own paws from sheer hunger. The Shepherd felt that if he once removed his eyes off the beast he was a dead man, and in order to keep himself awake he made songs and sang them, and so the night went by.

Next morning the Lord Chamberlain came to see the Shepherd's bones, and was amazed to find him alive and well. He led him to the King, who fell into a furious passion, and said:

"Well, you have learned what it is to be very near death, and now will you say, 'To my very good health'?"

But the Shepherd answered:

"I am not afraid of ten deaths! I will only say it if I may have the Princess for my wife."

"Then go to your death," cried the King, and ordered him to be thrown into the den with the wild boars.

The wild boars had not been fed for a week, and when the Shepherd was thrust into their den they rushed at him to tear him to pieces. But the Shepherd took a little flute out of the sleeve of his jacket, and began to play a merry tune, on which the wild boars first of all shrank shyly away, and then got up on their hind legs and danced gaily. The Shepherd would have given anything to be able to laugh, they looked so funny; but he dared not stop playing, for he knew well enough that the moment he stopped they would fall upon him and tear him to pieces. His eyes were of no use to him here, for he could not have stared ten wild boars in the face at once; so he kept on playing, and the wild boars danced very slowly, as if in a minuet; then by degrees he played faster and faster, till they could hardly twist and turn quickly enough, and ended by all falling over each other in a heap, quite exhausted and out of breath.

Then the Shepherd ventured to laugh at last; and he laughed so long and so loud that when the Lord Chamberlain came early in the morning, expecting to find only his bones, the tears were still running down his cheeks from laughter.

As soon as the King was dressed the Shepherd was again brought before him; but he was more angry than ever to think the wild boars had not torn the man to bits, and he said:

"Well, you have learned what it feels to be near ten deaths, *now* say 'To my good health!' "

But the Shepherd broke in with:

"I do not fear a hundred deaths; and I will only say it if I may have the Princess for my wife."

"Then go to a hundred deaths!" roared the King, and ordered the Shepherd to be thrown down the deep vault of scythes.

The guards dragged him away to a dark dungeon, in the middle of which was a deep well with sharp scythes all round it. At the bottom of the well was a little light by which one could see, if any-one was thrown in, whether he had fallen to the bottom.

When the Shepherd was dragged to the dungeon he begged the guards to leave him alone a little while that he might look down into the pit of scythes; perhaps he might after all make up his mind to say, "To your good health" to the King.

So the guards left him alone, and he stuck up his long stick near the wall, hung his cloak round the stick and put his hat on the top. He also hung his knapsack up beside the cloak, so that it might seem to have some body within it. When this was done, he called out to the guards and said that he had considered the matter, but after all he could not make up his mind to say what the King wished.

The guards came in, threw the hat and cloak, knapsack and stick all down in the well together, watched to see how they put out the light at the bottom, and came away, thinking that now there was really an end of the Shepherd. But he had hidden in a dark corner, and was now laughing to himself all the time.

Quite early next morning came the Lord Chamberlain with a lamp, and he nearly fell backwards with surprise when he saw the Shepherd alive and well. He brought him to the King, whose fury was greater than ever, but who cried:

"Well, now you have been near a hundred deaths; will you say, 'To your good health'?"

But the Shepherd only gave the same answer:

"I won't say it till the Princess is my wife."

"Perhaps, after all, you may do it for less," said the King, who saw that there was no chance of making away with the Shepherd; and he ordered the state coach to be got ready; then he made the Shepherd get in with him and sit beside him, and ordered the coachman to drive to the silver wood.

When they reached it, he said:

"Do you see this silver wood? Well, if you will say 'To your good health,' I will give it to you."

The Shepherd turned hot and cold by turns, but he still persisted:

"I will not say it till the Princess is my wife."

The King was much vexed; he drove further on till they came to a splendid castle, all of gold, and then he said:

"Do you see this golden castle? Well, I will give you that too, the silver wood and the golden castle, if only you will say that one thing to me: 'To your good health.'"

The Shepherd gaped and wondered, and was quite dazzled but he still said:

"No, I will not say it till I have the Princess for my wife."

This time the King was overwhelmed with grief, and gave orders to drive on to the diamond pond, and there he tried once more:

"You shall have them all—all, if you will but say 'To your good health.'"

The Shepherd had to shut his staring eyes tight

not to be dazzled with the brilliant pond, but still he said:

"No, no; I will not say it till I have the Princess for my wife."

Then the King saw that all his efforts were useless, and that he might as well give in; so he said:

"Well, well, it is all the same to me—I will give you my daughter to wife; but then you really and truly must say to me, 'To your good health.' "

"Of course I'll say it; why should I not say it? It stands to reason that I shall say it then."

At this the King was more delighted than anyone could have believed. He made it known all through the country that there were going to be great rejoicings, as the Princess was going to be married. And everyone rejoiced to think that the Princess, who had refused so many royal suitors, should have ended by falling in love with the staring-eyed Shepherd.

There was such a wedding as had never been seen. Everyone ate and drank and danced. Even the sick were feasted, and quite tiny new-born children had presents given them. But the greatest merrymaking was in the King's palace; there the best bands played and the best food was cooked. A crowd of people sat down to table, and all was fun and merrymaking.

And when the groomsman, according to custom, brought in the great boar's head on a big dish and placed it before the King, so that he might carve it and give everyone a share, the savoury smell was so strong that the King began to sneeze with all his might.

"To your very good health!" cried the Shepherd before anyone else, and the King was so delighted that he did not regret having given him his daughter.

In time, when the old King died, the Shepherd succeeded him. He made a very good king, and never expected his people to wish him well against their wills: but, all the same, everyone did wish him well, because they loved him.

THE PROUD COCK

There was once a cock who grew so dreadfully proud that he would have nothing to say to anybody. He left his house, it being far beneath his dignity to have any trammel of that sort in his life, and as for his former acquaintance, he cut them all.

One day, whilst walking about, he came to a few little sparks of fire which were nearly dead.

They cried out to him: "Please fan us with your wings, and we shall come to the full vigour of life again."

But he did not deign to answer, and as he was going away one of the sparks said: "Ah well! we shall die, but our big brother, the Fire, will pay you out for this one day."

On another day he was airing himself in a meadow, showing himself off in a very superb set of clothes. A voice calling from somewhere said: "Please be so good as to drop us into the water again."

He looked about and saw a few drops of water: they had got separated from their friends in the river, and were pining away with grief. "Oh! please be so good as to drop us into the water again," they said; but, without any answer, he drank up the drops. He was too proud and a great deal too big to talk to a poor little puddle of water; but the drops said: "Our big brother, the Water, will one day take you in hand, you proud and senseless creature."

Some days afterwards, during a great storm of rain, thunder and lightning, the cock took shelter in a little empty cottage, and shut to the door; and he thought: "I am clever; I am in comfort. What fools people are to stop out in a storm like this! What's that?" thought he. "I never heard a sound like that before."

In a little while it grew much louder, and when a few minutes had passed, it was a perfect howl. "Oh!" thought he, "this well never do. I must stop it somehow. But what is it I have to stop?"

He soon found it was the wind, shouting through the keyhole, so he plugged up the keyhole with a bit of clay, and then the wind was able to rest. He was very tired with whistling so long through the keyhole, and he said: "Now, if ever I have at any time a chance of doing a good turn to that princely domestic fowl, I will do it."

Weeks afterwards, the cock looked in at a house door: he seldom went there, because the miser to whom the house belonged almost starved himself, and so, of course, there was nothing over for anybody else.

To his amazement the cock saw the miser bending over a pot on the fire. At last the old fellow turned round to get a spoon with which to stir his pot, and then the cock, waking up, looked in and saw that the miser was making oyster-soup, for he had found some oyster-shells in an ash-pit, and to give the mixture a colour he had put in a few halfpence in the pot.

The miser chanced to turn quickly round, while the cock was peering into the saucepan, and, chuckling to himself, he said: "I shall have some chicken broth after all."

He tripped up the cock into the pot and shut the lid on. The bird, feeling warm, said: "Water, water, don't boil!" But the water only said: "You drank up my young brothers once: don't ask a favour of *me*."

Then he called out to the Fire: "Oh! kind Fire, don't boil the water." But the Fire replied: "You once let my young sisters die: you cannot expect any mercy from me." So he flared up and boiled the water all the faster.

At last, when the cock got unpleasantly warm, he thought of the wind, and called out: "Oh, Wind, come to my help!" and the Wind said: "Why, there is that noble domestic bird in trouble. I will help him." So he came down the chimney, blew out the fire, blew the lid off the pot, and blew the cock far away into the air, and at last settled him on a steeple, where the cock has remained ever since. And people say that the halfpence which were in the pot when it was boiling have given him the queer brown colour he still wears.

From the Spanish.

SNEGOURKA

There lived once, in Russia, a peasant and his wife who would have been as happy as the day is long, if only God had given them a little child.

One day, as they were watching the children playing in the snow, the man said to the woman:

"Wife, shall we go out and help the children make a snowball?"

But the wife answered, smiling:

"Nay, husband, but since God has given us no little child, let us go and fashion one from the snow."

And she put on her long blue cloak, and he put on his long brown coat, and they went out onto the crisp snow, and began to fashion the little child.

First, they made the feet and the legs and the little body, and then they took a ball of snow for the head. And at that moment a stranger in a long cloak, with his hat well drawn over his face, passed that way, and said: "Heaven help your undertaking!"

And the peasants crossed themselves and said: "It is well to ask help from Heaven in all we do."

Then they went on fashioning the little child. And they made two holes for the eyes and formed the nose and the mouth. And then—wonder of wonders—the little child came alive, and breath came from its nostrils and parted lips.

And the man was afeared, and said to his wife: "What have we done?"

And the wife said: "This is the little girl child God has sent us." And she gathered it into her arms, and the loose snow fell away from the little creature. Her hair became golden and her eyes were as blue as forget-me-nots—but there was no colour in her cheeks, because there was no blood in her veins.

In a few days she was like a child of three or four, and in a few weeks she seemed to be the age of nine or ten, and ran about gaily and prattled with the other children, who loved her so dearly, though she was so different from them.

Only, happy as she was, and dearly as her parents loved her, there was one terror in her life, and that was the sun. And during the day she would run and hide herself in cool, damp places away from the sunshine, and this the other children could not understand.

As the Spring advanced and the days grew longer and warmer, little Snegourka (for this was the name by which she was known) grew paler and thinner, and her mother would often ask her:

"What ails you, my darling?" and Snegourka would say: "Nothing, Mother, but I wish the sun were not so bright."

One day, on St. John's Day, the children of the village came to fetch her for a day in the woods, and they gathered flowers for her and did all they could to make her happy, but it was only when the great red sun went down that Snegourka drew a deep breath of relief and spread her little hands out to the cool evening air. And the boys, glad at her gladness, said: "Let us do something for Snegourka. Let us light a bonfire." And Snegourka not knowing what a bonfire was, she clapped her hands and was as merry and eager as they. And she helped them gather the sticks, and then they all stood round the pile and the boys set fire to the wood.

Snegourka stood watching the flames and listening to the crackle of the wood; and then suddenly they heard a tiny sound—and looking at the place where Snegourka had been standing, they saw nothing but a little snow-drift fast melting. And they called and called, "Snegourka! Snegourka!" thinking she had run into the forest. But there was no answer. Snegourka had disappeared from this life as mysteriously as she had come into it.

Adapted by M. L. Shedlock.

The river was so clear because it was the home of a very beautiful Water Nixie who lived in it, and who sometimes could emerge from her home and sit in woman's form upon the bank. She had a dark green smock upon her, the colour of the water-weed that waves as the water wills it, deep, deep down. And in her long wet hair were the white flowers of the water-violet, and she held a reed mace in her hand. Her face was very sad, because she had lived a long life, and known so many adventures, ever since she was a baby, which was nearly a hundred years ago. For creatures of the streams and trees live a long, long time, and when they die they lose themselves in Nature. That means that they are forever clouds, or trees, or rivers, and never have the form of men and women again.

All water creatures would live, if they might choose it, in the sea, where they are born. It is in the sea they float hand-in-hand upon the crested billows, and sink deep in the great troughs of the strong waves, that are green as jade. They follow the foam and lose themselves in the wide ocean—

> "Where great whales come sailing by,
> Sail and sail with unshut eye;"

and they store in the Sea King's palace the golden phosphor of the sea. But this Water Nixie had lost her happiness through not being good. She had forgotten many things that had been told her, and she had done many things that grieved others. She had stolen somebody else's property—quite a large bundle of happiness—which belonged elsewhere and not to her. Happiness is generally made to fit the person who owns it, just as do your shoes, or clothes; so that when you take someone else's it's very little good to you, for it fits badly, and you can never forget it isn't yours.

So what with one thing and another, this Water Nixie had to be punished, and the Queen of the Sea had banished her from the waves.[1]

"You shall live for a long time in little places, where you will weary of yourself. You will learn to know yourself so well that everything you want will seem too good for you, and you will cease to claim it. And so, in time, you shall get free."

Then the Nixie had to rise up and go away,

[1] "The punishment that can most affect Merfolk is to restrict their freedom. And this is how the Queen of the Sea punished the Nixie of our tale."

and be shut into the fastness of a very small space, according to the words of the Queen. And this small space was—a tear.

At first she could hardly express her misery, and by thinking so continuously of the wideness and savour of the sea, she brought a dash of the brine with her, that makes the saltness of our tears. She became many times smaller than her own stature; even then, by standing upright and spreading wide her arms, she touched with her finger-tips the walls of her tiny crystal home. How she longed that this tear might be wept, and the walls of her prison shattered! But the owner of this tear was of a very proud nature, and she was so sad that tears seemed to her in no wise to express her grief.

She was a Princess who lived in a country that was not her home. What were tears to her? If she could have stood on the top of the very highest hill and with both hands caught the great winds of heaven, strong as they, and striven with them, perhaps she might have felt as if she expressed all she knew. Or, if she could have torn down the stars from the heavens, or cast her mantle over the sun. But tears! Would they have helped to tell her sorrow? You cry if you soil your copy-book, don't you? or pinch your hand? So you may imagine the Nixie's home was a safe one, and she turned round and round in the captivity of that tear.

For twenty years she dwelt in that strong heart, till she grew to be accustomed to her cell. At last, in this wise came her release.

An old gipsy came one morning to the Castle and begged to see the Princess. She must see her, she cried. And the Princess came down the steps to meet her, and the gipsy gave her a small roll of paper in her hand. And the roll of paper smelt like honey as she took it, and it adhered to her palm as she opened it. There was little sign of writing on the paper, but in the midst of the page was a picture, small as the picture reflected in the iris of an eye. The picture shewed a hill, with one tree on the sky-line, and a long road wound round the hill.

And suddenly in the Princess' memory a voice spoke to her. Many sounds she heard, gathered up into one great silence, like the quiet there is in forest spaces, when it is Summer and the green is deep:—

> "Blessed are they that have the home longing,
> For they shall go home."

Then the Princess gave the gipsy two golden pieces, and went up to her chamber, and long that night she sat, looking out upon the sky.

She had no need to look upon the honeyed scroll, though she held it closely. Clearly before her did she see that small picture: the hill, and the tree, and the winding road, imaged as if mirrored in the iris of an eye. And in her memory she was upon that road, and the hill rose beside her, and the little tree was outlined, every twig of it, against the sky.

And as she saw all this, an overwhelming love of the place arose in her, a love of that certain bit of country that was so sharp and strong, that it stung and swayed her, as she leaned on the window-sill.

And because the love of a country is one of the deepest loves you may feel, the band of her control was loosened, and the tears came welling to her eyes. Up they brimmed and over in salty rush and follow, dimming her eyes, magnifying everything, speared for a moment on her eyelashes, then shimmering to their fall. And at last came the tear that held the disobedient Nixie.

Splish! it fell. And she was free.

If you could have seen how pretty she looked standing there, about the height of a grass-blade, wringing out her long wet hair. Every bit of moisture she wrung out of it, she was so glad to be quit of that tear. Then she raised her two arms above her in one delicious stretch, and if you had been the size of a mustard-seed perhaps you might have heard her laughing. Then she grew a little, and grew and grew, till she was about the height of a bluebell, and as slender to see.

She stood looking at the splash on the window-sill that had been her prison so long, and then, with three steps of her bare feet, she reached the jessamine that was growing by the window, and by this she swung herself to the ground.

Away she sped over the dew-drenched meadows till she came to the running brook, and with all her longing in her outstretched hands, she kneeled down by the crooked willows among all the comfry and the loosestrife, and the yellow irises and the reeds.

Then she slid into the wide, cool stream.

From *The Children and the Pictures,* by Pamela Tennant (Lady Glenconner).

THE BLUE ROSE

There lived once upon a time in China a wise Emperor who had one daughter. His daughter was remarkable for her perfect beauty. Her feet were the smallest in the world; her eyes were long and slanting and bright as brown onyxes, and when you heard her laugh it was like listening to a tinkling stream or to the chimes of a silver bell. Moreover, the Emperor's daughter was as wise as she was beautiful, and she chanted the verse of the great poets better than anyone in the land. The Emperor was old in years; his son was married and had begotten a son; he was, therefore, quite happy with regard to the succession to the throne, but he wished before he died to see his daughter wedded to someone who should be worthy of her.

Many suitors presented themselves to the palace as soon as it became known that the Emperor desired a son-in-law, but when they reached the palace they were met by the Lord Chamberlain, who told them that the Emperor had decided that only the man who found and brought back the blue rose should marry his daughter. The suitors were much puzzled by this order. What was the blue rose and where was it to be found? In all, a hundred and fifty suitors had presented themselves, and out of these fifty at once put away from them all thought of winning the hand of the Emperor's daughter, since they considered the condition imposed to be absurd.

The other hundred set about trying to find the blue rose. One of them—his name was Ti-Fun-Ti—he was a merchant and was immensely rich, at once went to the largest shop in the town and said to the shopkeeper, "I want a blue rose, the best you have."

The shopkeeper, with many apologies, explained that he did not stock blue roses. He had red roses in profusion, white, pink, and yellow roses, but no blue roses. There had hitherto been no demand for the article.

"Well," said Ti-Fun-Ti, "you must get one for me. I do not mind how much money it costs, but I must have a blue rose."

The shopkeeper said he would do his best, but he feared it would be an expensive article and difficult to procure. Another of the suitors, whose name I have forgotten, was a warrior, and extremely brave; he mounted his horse, and taking with him a hundred archers and a thousand horsemen, he marched into the territory of the King of the Five Rivers, whom he knew to be the richest king in the world and the possessor of the rarest treasures, and demanded of him the blue rose, threatening him with a terrible doom should he be reluctant to give it up.

The King of the Five Rivers, who disliked soldiers, and had a horror of noise, physical violence, and every kind of fuss (his bodyguard was armed solely with fans and sunshades), rose from the cushions on which he was lying when the demand was made, and, tinkling a small bell, said to the servant who straightway appeared, "Fetch me the blue rose."

The servant retired and returned presently bearing on a silken cushion a large sapphire which was carved so as to imitate a full-blown rose with all its petals.

"This," said the King of the Five Rivers, "is the blue rose. You are welcome to it."

The warrior took it, and after making brief, soldier-like thanks, he went straight back to the Emperor's palace, saying that he had lost no time in finding the blue rose. He was ushered into the presence of the Emperor, who as soon as he heard the warrior's story and saw the blue rose which had been brought sent for his daughter and said to her: "This intrepid warrior has brought you what he claims to be the blue rose. Has he accomplished the quest?"

The Princess took the precious object in her

hands, and after examining it for a moment, said: "This is not a rose at all. It is a sapphire; I have no need of precious stones." And she returned the stone to the warrior with many elegantly expressed thanks. And the warrior went away in discomfiture.

The merchant, hearing of the warrior's failure, was all the more anxious to win the prize. He sought the shopkeeper and said to him: "Have you got me the blue rose? I trust you have; because, if not, I shall most assuredly be the means of your death. My brother-in-law is chief magistrate, and I am allied by marriage to all the chief officials in the kingdom."

The shopkeeper turned pale and said: "Sir, give me three days and I will procure you the rose without fail." The merchant granted him the three days and went away. Now the shopkeeper was at his wit's end as to what to do, for he knew well there was no such thing as a blue rose. For two days he did nothing but moan and wring his hands, and on the third day he went to his wife and said, "Wife, we are ruined."

But his wife, who was a sensible woman, said: "Nonsense. If there is no such thing as a blue rose we must make one. Go to the chemist and ask him for a strong dye which will change a white rose into a blue one."

So the shopkeeper went to the chemist and asked

him for a dye, and the chemist gave him a bottle of red liquid, telling him to pick a white rose and to dip its stalk into the liquid and the rose would turn blue. The shopkeeper did as he was told; the rose turned into a beautiful blue and the shopkeeper took it to the merchant, who at once went with it to the palace saying that he had found the blue rose.

He was ushered into the presence of the Emperor, who as soon as he saw the blue rose sent for his daughter and said to her: "This wealthy merchant has brought you what he claims to be the blue rose. Has he accomplished the quest?"

The Princess took the flower in her hands and after examining it for a moment said: "This is a white rose, its stalk has been dipped in a poisonous dye and it has turned blue. Were a butterfly to settle upon it it would die of the potent fume. Take it back. I have no need of a dyed rose." And she returned it to the merchant with many elegantly expressed thanks.

The other ninety-eight suitors all sought in various ways for the blue rose. Some of them traveled all over the world seeking it; some of them sought the aid of wizards and astrologers, and one did not hesitate to invoke the help of the dwarfs that live underground; but all of them, whether they traveled in far countries or took counsel with wizards and demons or sat pondering in lonely places, failed to find the blue rose.

At last they all abandoned the quest except the Lord Chief Justice, who was the most skillful lawyer and statesman in the country. After thinking over the matter for several months he sent for the most famous artist in the country and said to him: "Make me a china cup. Let it be milk-white in colour and perfect in shape, and paint on it a rose, a blue rose."

The artist made obeisance and withdrew, and worked for two months at the Lord Chief Justice's cup. In two months' time it was finished, and the world has never seen such a beautiful cup, so perfect in symmetry, so delicate in texture, and the rose on it, the blue rose, was a living flower, picked in fairyland and floating on the rare milky surface of the porcelain. When the Lord Chief Justice saw it he gasped with surprise and pleasure, for he was a great lover of porcelain, and never in his life had he seen such a piece. He said to himself, "Without doubt the blue rose is here on this cup and nowhere else."

So, after handsomely rewarding the artist, he went to the Emperor's palace and said that he had brought the blue rose. He was ushered into the Emperor's presence, who as he saw the cup sent for his daughter and said to her: "This eminent lawyer has brought you what he claims to be the blue rose. Has he accomplished the quest?"

The Princess took the bowl in her hands, and after examining it for a moment said: "This bowl is the most beautiful piece of china I have ever seen. If you are kind enough to let me keep it I will put it aside until I receive the blue rose. For so beautiful is it that no other flower is worthy to be put in it except the blue rose."

The Lord Chief Justice thanked the Princess for accepting the bowl with many elegantly turned phrases, and he went away in discomfiture.

After this there was no one in the whole country who ventured on the quest of the blue rose. It happened that not long after the Lord Chief Justice's attempt a strolling minstrel visited the kingdom of the Emperor. One evening he was playing his one-stringed instrument outside a dark wall. It was a summer's evening, and the sun had sunk in a glory of dusty gold, and in the violet twilight one or two stars were twinkling like spear-heads. There was an incessant noise made by the croaking of frogs and the chatter of grasshoppers. The minstrel was singing a short song over and over again to a monotonous tune. The sense of it was something like this:

I watched beside the willow trees
  The river, as the evening fell,
The twilight came and brought no breeze,
  Nor dew, nor water for the well.

When from the tangled banks of grass
A bird across the water flew,
And in the river's hard grey glass
I saw a flash of azure blue.

As he sang he heard a rustle on the wall, and looking up he saw a slight figure white against the twilight, beckoning to him. He walked along under the wall until he came to a gate, and there someone was waiting for him, and he was gently led into the shadow of a dark cedar tree. In the dim twilight he saw two bright eyes looking at him, and he understood their message. In the twilight a thousand meaningless nothings were whispered in the light of the stars, and the hours fled swiftly. When the East began to grow light, the Princess (for it was she) said it was time to go.

"But," said the minstrel, "to-morrow I shall come to the palace and ask for your hand."

"Alas!" said the Princess, "I would that were possible, but my father has made a foolish condition that only he may wed me who finds the blue rose."

"That is simple," said the minstrel. "I will find it." And they said good night to each other.

The next morning the minstrel went to the palace, and on his way he picked a common white rose from a wayside garden. He was ushered into the Emperor's presence, who sent for his daughter and said to her: "This penniless minstrel has brought you what he claims to be the blue rose. Has he accomplished the quest?"

The Princess took the rose in her hands and said: "Yes, this is without doubt the blue rose."

But the Lord Chief Justice and all who were present respectfully pointed out that the rose was a common white rose and not a blue one, and the objection was with many forms and phrases conveyed to the Princess.

"I think the rose is blue," said the Princess. "Perhaps you are all colour blind."

The Emperor, with whom the decision rested, decided that if the Princess thought the rose was blue it was blue, for it was well known that her perception was more acute than that of any one else in the kingdom.

So the minstrel married the Princess, and they settled on the sea coast in a little seen house with a garden full of white roses, and they lived happily for ever afterwards. And the Emperor, knowing that his daughter had made a good match, died in peace.

By Maurice Baring.

THE TWO FROGS

Once upon a time in the country of Japan there lived two frogs, one of whom made his home in a ditch near the town of Osaka, on the sea coast, while the other dwelt in a clear little stream which ran through the city of Kioto. At such a great distance apart, they had never even heard of each other; but, funnily enough, the idea came into both their heads at once that they should like to see a little of the world, and the frog who lived at Kioto wanted to visit Osaka, and the frog who lived at Osaka wished to go to Kioto, where the great Mikado had his palace.

So one fine morning in the spring, they both set out along the road that led from Kioto to Osaka, one from one end and the other from the other.

The journey was more tiring than they expected, for they did not know much about travelling, and half-way between the two towns there rose a mountain which had to be climbed. It took them a long time and a great many hops to reach the top, but there they were at last, and what was the surprise of each to see another frog before him! They looked at each other for a moment without speaking, and then fell into conversation, and explained the cause of their meeting so far from their homes. It was delightful to find that they both felt the same wish—to learn a little more of their native country—and as there was no sort of hurry they stretched themselves out in a cool, damp place, and agreed that they would have a good rest before they parted to go their ways.

"What a pity we are not bigger," said the Osaka frog, "and then we could see both towns from here and tell if it is worth our while going on."

"Oh, that is easily managed," returned the Kioto frog. "We have only got to stand up on our hind legs, and hold on to each other, and then we can each look at the town he is travelling to."

This idea pleased the Osaka frog so much that he at once jumped up and put his front paws on the shoulder of his friend, who had risen also. There they both stood, stretching themselves as high as they could, and holding each other tightly, so that they might not fall down. The Kioto frog turned his nose towards Osaka, and the Osaka frog turned his nose towards Kioto; but the foolish things forgot that when they stood up their great eyes lay in the backs of their heads, and that though their noses might point to the places to which they wanted to go, their eyes beheld the places from which they had come.

"Dear me!" cried the Osaka frog; "Kioto is exactly like Osaka. It is certainly not worth such a long journey. I shall go home."

"If I had had any idea that Osaka was only a copy of Kioto I should never have travelled all this way," exclaimed the frog from Kioto, and as he spoke, he took his hands from his friend's shoulders and they both fell down on the grass.

Then they took a polite farewell of each other, and set off for home again, and to the end of their lives they believed that Osaka and Kioto, which are as different to look at as two towns can be, were as like as two peas.

From *The Violet Fairy Book,* by Andrew Lang.

THE WISE OLD SHEPHERD

Once upon a time a Snake went out of his hole to take an airing. He crawled about, greatly enjoying the scenery and the fresh whiff of the breeze, until, seeing an open door, he went in. Now this door was the door of the palace of the King, and inside was the King himself, with all his courtiers.

Imagine their horror at seeing a huge Snake crawling in at the door. They all ran away except the King, who felt that his rank forbade him to be a coward, and the King's son. The King called out for somebody to come and kill the Snake; but this horrified them still more, because in that country the people believed it to be wicked to kill any living thing, even snakes and scorpions and wasps. So the courtiers did nothing, but the young Prince obeyed his father, and killed the Snake with his stick.

After a while the Snake's wife became anxious and set out in search of her husband. She too saw the open door of the palace, and in she went. O horror! there on the floor lay the body of her husband, all covered with blood and quite dead. No one saw the Snake's wife crawl in; she inquired of a white ant what had happened, and when she found that the young Prince had killed her husband, she made a vow that, as he had made her a widow, so she would make his wife a widow.

That night, when all the world was asleep, the Snake crept into the Prince's bedroom, and coiled round his neck. The Prince slept on, and when he awoke in the morning, he was surprised to find his neck encircled with the coils of a snake. He was afraid to stir, so there he remained, until the Prince's mother became anxious and went to see what was the matter. When she entered his room, and saw him in this plight, she gave a loud shriek, and ran off to tell the King.

"Call the archers," said the King.

The archers came, and the King told them to go to the Prince's room, and shoot the Snake that was coiled about his neck. They were so clever, that they could easily do this without hurting the Prince at all.

In came the archers in a row, fitted the arrows to the bows, the bows were raised and ready to shoot, when, on a sudden, from the Snake there issued a voice which spoke as follows:

"O archers, wait, wait and hear me before you shoot. It is not fair to carry out the sentence before you have heard the case. Is not this a good law: an eye for an eye, and a tooth for a tooth? Is it not so, O King?"

"Yes," replied the King, "that is our law."

"Then," said the Snake, "I plead the law. Your son has made me a widow, so it is fair and right that I should make his wife a widow."

"That sounds right enough," said the King, "but right and law are not always the same thing. We had better ask somebody who knows."

They asked all the judges, but none of them could tell the law of the matter. They shook their heads, and said they would look up all their law-books, and see whether anything of the sort had ever happened before, and if so, how it had been decided. That is the way judges used to decide cases in that country, though I dare say it sounds to you a very funny way. It looked as if they had not much sense in their own heads, and perhaps that was true. The upshot of it all was that not a judge would give an opinion; so the King sent messengers all over the countryside, to see if they could find somebody somewhere who knew something.

One of these messengers found a party of five shepherds, who were sitting upon a hill and trying to decide a quarrel of their own. They gave their opinions so freely, and in language so very strong, that the King's messenger said to himself, "Here are the men for us. Here are five men, each with an opinion of his own, and all different." Post-haste he scurried back to the King, and told him that he had found at last some one ready to judge the knotty point.

So the King and the Queen, and the Prince and Princess, and all the courtiers, got on horseback, and away they galloped to the hill whereupon the five shepherds were sitting, and the Snake too went with them, coiled round the neck of the Prince.

When they got to the shepherds' hill, the shepherds were dreadfully frightened. At first they thought that the strangers were a gang of robbers, and when they saw it was the King their next thought was that one of their misdeeds had been found out; and each of them began thinking what was the last thing he had done, and wondering, was it that?

But the King and the courtiers got off their horses, and said good day, in the most civil way. So the shepherds felt their minds set at ease again. Then the King said:

"Worthy shepherds, we have a question to put to you, which not all the judges in all the courts of my city have been able to solve. Here is my son, and here, as you see, is a snake coiled round his neck. Now, the husband of this Snake came creeping into my palace hall, and my son the Prince killed him; so this Snake, who is the wife of the other, says that, as my son has made her a widow, so she has a right to widow my son's wife. What do you think about it?"

The first shepherd said: "I think she is quite right, my Lord the King. If anyone made my wife a widow, I would pretty soon do the same to him."

This was brave language, and the other shepherds shook their heads and looked fierce. But the King was puzzled, and could not quite understand it. You see, in the first place, if the man's wife were a widow, the man would be dead; and then it is hard to see that he could do anything. So, to make sure, the King asked the second shepherd whether that was his opinion too.

"Yes," said the second shepherd; "now the Prince has killed the Snake, the Snake has a right to kill the Prince if he can." But that was not of much use either, as the Snake was as dead as a doornail. So the King passed on to the third.

"I agree with my mates," said the third shepherd. "Because, you see, a Prince is a Prince, but then a Snake is a Snake." That was quite true, they all admitted, but it did not seem to help the matter much. Then the King asked the fourth shepherd to say what he thought.

The fourth shepherd said: "An eye for an eye, and a tooth for a tooth; so I think a widow should be a widow, if so be she don't marry again."

By this time the poor King was so puzzled that he hardly knew whether he stood on his head or his heels. But there was still the fifth shepherd left; the oldest and wisest of them all; and the fifth shepherd said:

"King, I should like to ask two questions."

"Ask twenty, if you like," said the King. He did not promise to answer them, so he could afford to be generous.

"First. I ask the Princess how many sons she has."

"Four," said the Princess.

"And how many sons has Mistress Snake here?"

"Seven," said the Snake.

"Then," said the old shepherd, "it will be quite fair for Mistress Snake to kill his Highness the Prince when her Highness the Princess has had three sons more."

"I never thought of that," said the Snake. "Good-bye, King, and all you good people. Send a message when the Princess has had three more sons, and you may count upon me—I will not fail you."

So saying, she uncoiled from the Prince's neck and slid away among the grass.

The King and the Prince and everybody shook hands with the wise old shepherd, and went home again. And the Princess never had any more sons at all. She and the Prince lived happily for many years; and if they are not dead they are living still.

From *The Talking Thrush,* by W. H. D. Rouse.

THE FOLLY OF PANIC

And it came to pass that the Buddha (to be) was born again as a Lion. Just as he had helped his fellow-men, he now began to help his fellow-animals, and there was a great deal to be done. For instance, there was a little nervous Hare who was always afraid that something dreadful was going to happen to her. She was always saying: "Suppose the Earth were to fall in, what would happen to me?" And she said this so often that at last she thought it really was about to happen. One day, when she had been saying over and over again, "Suppose the Earth were to fall in, what would happen to me?" she heard a slight noise: it really was only a heavy fruit which had fallen upon a rustling leaf, but the little Hare was so nervous she was ready to believe anything, and she said in a frightened tone: "The Earth *is* falling in." She ran away as fast as she could go, and presently she met an old brother Hare, who said: "Where are you running to, Mistress Hare?"

And the little Hare said: "I have no time to stop and tell you anything. The Earth is falling in, and I am running away."

"The Earth is falling in, is it?" said the old brother Hare, in a tone of much astonishment; and he repeated this to *his* brother hare, and *he* to *his* brother hare, and he to *his* brother hare, until at last there were a hundred thousand brother hares, all shouting: "The Earth is falling in." Now presently the bigger animals began to take the cry up. First the deer, and then the sheep, and then the wild boar, and then the buffalo, and then the camel, and then the tiger, and then the elephant.

Now the wise Lion heard all this noise and wondered at it. "There are no signs," he said, "of the Earth falling in. They must have heard something." And then he stopped them all short and said: "What is this you are saying?"

And the Elephant said: "I remarked that the Earth was falling in."

"How do you know this?" asked the Lion.

"Why, now I come to think of it, it was the Tiger that remarked it to me."

And the Tiger said: "I had it from the Camel," and the Camel said: "I had it from the Buffalo." And the buffalo from the wild boar, and the wild boar from the sheep, and the sheep from the deer, and the deer from the hares, and the Hares said: "Oh! *we* heard it from *that* little Hare."

And the Lion said: "Little Hare, *what* made you say that the Earth was falling in?"

And the little Hare said: "I *saw* it."

"You saw it?" said the Lion. "Where?"

"Yonder, by that tree."

"Well," said the Lion, "come with me and I will show you how——"

"No, no," said the Hare, "I would not go near that tree for anything, I'm *so* nervous."

"But," said the Lion, "I am going to take you on my back." And he took her on his back, and begged the animals to stay where they were until they returned. Then he showed the little Hare how the fruit had fallen upon the leaf, making the noise that had frightened her, and she said: "Yes, I see—the Earth is *not* falling in." And the Lion said: "Shall we go back and tell the other animals?" And they went back. The little Hare stood before the animals and said: "The Earth is *not* falling in." And all the animals began to repeat this to one another, and they dispersed gradually, and you heard the words more and more softly:

"The Earth is *not* falling in," etc., etc., etc., until the sound died away altogether.

From *Eastern Stories and Legends.*

NOTE.—This story I have told in my own words, using the language I have found most effective for very young children.

THE TRUE SPIRIT OF A FESTIVAL DAY

And it came to pass that the Buddha was born a Hare and lived in a wood; on one side was the foot of a mountain, on another a river, on the third side a border village.

And with him lived three friends: a Monkey, a Jackal and an Otter; each of these creatures got food on his own hunting ground. In the evening they met together, and the Hare taught his companions many wise things: that the moral law should be observed, that alms should be given to the poor, and that holy days should be kept.

One day the Buddha said: "To-morrow is a fast day. Feed any beggars that come to you by giving food from your own table." They all consented.

The next day the Otter went down to the bank of the Ganges to seek his prey. Now a fisherman had landed seven red fish and had buried them in the sand on the river's bank while he went down the stream catching more fish. The Otter scented the buried fish, dug up the sand till he came upon them, and he called aloud: "Does any one own these fish?" And, not seeing the owner, he laid the fish in the jungle where he dwelt, intending to eat them at a fitting time. Then he lay down, thinking how virtuous he was.

The Jackal also went off in search of food, and found in the hut of a field watcher a lizard, two spits, and a pot of milk-curd.

And, after thrice crying aloud, "To whom do these belong?" and not finding an owner, he put on his neck the rope for lifting the pot, and grasping the spits and lizard with his teeth, he laid them in his own lair, thinking, "In due season I will devour them," and then he lay down, thinking how virtuous he had been.

The Monkey entered the clump of trees, and gathering a bunch of mangoes, laid them up in his part of the jungle, meaning to eat them in due season. He then lay down and thought how virtuous he had been.

But the Hare (who was the Buddha-to-be) in due time came out, thinking to lie (in contemplation) on the Kuca grass. "It is impossible for me to offer *grass* to any beggars who may chance to come by, and I have no oil or rice or fish. If any beggar come to me, I will give him (of) my own flesh to eat."

Now when Sakka, the King of the Gods, heard this thing, he determined to put the Royal Hare to the test. So he came in disguise of a Brahmin to the Otter and said: "Wise Sir, if I could get something to eat, I would perform *all* my priestly duties."

The Otter said: "I will give you food. Seven red fish have I safely brought to land from the sacred river of the Ganges. Eat thy fill, O Brahmin, and stay in this wood."

And the Brahmin said: "Let it be until to-morrow, and I will see to it then."

Then he went to the Jackal, who confessed that he had stolen the food, but he begged the Brahmin to accept it and remain in the wood; but the Brahmin said: "Let it be until the morrow, and then I will see to it."

And he came to the Monkey, who offered him the mangoes, and the Brahmin answered in the same way.

Then the Brahmin went to the wise Hare, and the Hare said: "Behold, I will give you of my flesh to eat. But you must not take life on this holy day. When you have piled up the logs I will sacrifice myself by falling into the midst of the flames, and when my body is roasted you shall eat my flesh and perform all your priestly duties."

Now when Sakka heard these words he caused a heap of burning coals to appear, and the Wisdom Being, rising from the grass, came to the place, but before casting himself into the flames he shook himself, lest perchance there should be any insects in his coat who might suffer death. Then, offering his body as a free gift, he sprang up, and like a royal swan, lighting on a bed of lotus in an ecstasy of joy, he fell on the heap of live coals. But the flame failed even to heat the pores or the hair on the body of the Wisdom Being, and it was as if he had entered a region of frost. Then he addressed the Brahmin in these words: "Brahmin, the fire that you have kindled is icy cold; it fails to heat the pores of the hair on my body. What is the meaning of this?"

"O most wise Hare! I am Sakka, and have come to put your virtue to the test."

And the Buddha in a sweet voice said: "No god or man could find in me an unwillingness to die."

Then Sakka said: "O wise Hare, be thy virtue known to all the ages to come."

And seizing the mountain he squeezed out the juice and daubed on the moon the signs of the young hare.

Then he placed him back on the grass that he might continue his Sabbath meditation, and returned to Heaven.

And the four creatures lived together and kept the moral law.

From *Eastern Stories and Legends.*

FILIAL PIETY

Now it came to pass that the Buddha was reborn in the shape of a parrot, and he greatly excelled all other parrots in his strength and beauty. And when he was full grown his father, who had long been the leader of the flock in their flights to other climes, said to him: "My son, behold my strength is spent! Do thou lead the flock, for I am no longer able." And the Buddha said: "Behold, thou shalt rest. I will lead the birds." And the parrots rejoiced in the strength of their new leader, and willingly did they follow him. Now from that day on, the Buddha undertook to feed his parents, and would not consent that they should do any more work. Each day he led his flock to the Himalaya Hills, and when he had eaten his fill of the clumps of rice that grew there, he filled his beak with food for the dear parents who were waiting his return.

Now there was a man appointed to watch the rice-fields, and he did his best to drive the parrots away, but there seemed to be some secret power in the leader of this flock which the keeper could not overcome.

He noticed that the parrots ate their fill and then flew away, but that the Parrot-King not only satisfied his hunger, but carried away rice in his beak.

Now he feared there would be no rice left, and he went to his master, the Brahmin, to tell him what had happened; and even as the master listened there came to him the thought that the Parrot-King was something higher than he seemed, and he loved him even before he saw him. But he said nothing of this, and only warned the Keeper that he should set a snare and catch the dangerous bird. So the man did as he was bidden: he made a small cage and set the snare, and sat down in his hut waiting for the birds to come. And soon he saw the Parrot-King amidst his flock, who, because he had no greed, sought no richer spot, but flew down to the same place in which he had fed the day before.

Now, no sooner had he touched the ground than he felt his feet caught in the noose. Then fear crept into his bird heart, but a stronger feeling was there to crush it down, for he thought: "If I cry out the Cry of the Captured, my Kinsfolk will be terrified, and they will fly away foodless. But if I lie still, then their hunger will be satisfied, and may they safely come to my aid." Thus, was the parrot both brave and prudent.

But alas! he did not know that his Kinsfolk had nought of his brave spirit. When *they* had eaten their fill, though they heard the thrice-uttered cry of the captured, they flew away, nor heeded the sad plight of their leader.

Then was the heart of the Parrot-King sore within him, and he said: "All these my kith and kin, and not one to look back on me. Alas! what sin have I done?"

The watchman now heard the cry of the Parrot-King, and the sound of the other parrots flying through the air. "What is that?" he cried, and leaving his hut he came to the place where he had laid the snare. There he found the captive parrot; he tied his feet together and brought him to the Brahmin, his master. Now, when the Brahmin saw the Parrot-King, he felt his strong power, and his heart was full of love to him, but he hid his feelings, and said in a voice of anger: "Is thy greed greater than that of all other birds? They eat their fill, but thou takest away each day more food than thou canst eat. Doest thou this out of hatred for me, or dost thou store up the food in some granary for selfish greed?"

And the Great Being made answer in a sweet human voice: "I hate thee not, O Brahmin. Nor do I store the rice in a granary for selfish greed. But this thing I do. Each day I pay a debt which is due—each day I grant a loan, and each day I store up a treasure."

Now the Brahmin could not understand the words of the Buddha (because true wisdom had not entered his heart) and he said: "I pray thee, O Wondrous Bird, to make these words clear unto me."

And then the Parrot-King made answer: "I carry food to my ancient parents who can no longer seek that food for themselves: thus I pay my daily debt. I carry food to my callow chicks whose wings are yet ungrown. When I am old they will care for me—this my loan to them. And for other birds, weak and helpless of wing, who need the aid of the strong, for them I lay up a store; to these I give in charity."

Then was the Brahmin much moved, and showed the love that was in his heart. "Eat thy fill, O Righteous Bird, and let thy Kinsfolk eat, too, for thy sake." And he wished to bestow a thousand acres of land upon him, but the Great Being would only take a tiny portion round which were set boundary stores.

And the parrot returned with a head of rice, and said: "Arise, dear parents, that I may take you to a place of plenty." And he told them the story of his deliverance.

From *Eastern Stories and Legends.*

THREE STORIES
FROM THE DANISH OF
HANS CHRISTIAN ANDERSEN

THREE STORIES FROM HANS CHRISTIAN ANDERSEN[1]

THE SWINEHERD

There was once a poor Prince. He owned a Kingdom—a very small one, but it was big enough to allow him to marry, and he was determined to marry. Now, it was really very bold on his part to say to an Emperor's daughter: "Will you marry me?" But he dared to do so, for his name was known far and wide, and there were hundreds of princesses who would willingly have said: "Yes, thank you." But, would *she?* We shall hear what happened.

On the grave of the Prince's father, there grew a rose-tree—such a wonderful rose-tree! It bloomed only once in five years, and then it bore only one rose—but what a rose! Its perfume was so sweet that whoever smelt it forgot all his cares and sorrows. The Prince had also a nightingale

[1] The three stories from Hans Christian Andersen have for so long formed part of my répertoire that I have been requested to include them. I am offering a free translation of my own from the Danish version.

which could sing as if all the delicious melodies in the world were contained in its little throat. The rose and the nightingale were both to be given to the Princess, and were therefore placed in two great silver caskets and sent to her. The Emperor had them carried before him into the great hall where the Princess was playing at "visiting" with her ladies-in-waiting—they had nothing else to do. When she saw the caskets with the presents in them, she clapped her hands with joy.

"If it were only a little pussy-cat," she cried. But out came a beautiful rose.

"How elegantly it is made," said all the ladies of the court.

"It is more than elegant," said the Emperor. "It is *neat.*"

"Fie, papa," she said, "it is not made at all; it is a *natural* rose."

"Let us see what the other casket contains before we lose our temper," said the Emperor, and then out came the little nightingale and sang so sweetly that at first nobody could think of anything to say against it.

"*Superbe, superbe,*" cried the ladies of the court, for they all chattered French, one worse than the other.

"How the bird reminds me of the late Empress' musical-box!" said an old Lord-in-Waiting. "Ah, me! the same tone, the same execution."

"The very same," said the Emperor, and he cried like a little child.

"I hope it is not a real bird," said the Princess.

"Oh, yes! it is a real bird," said those who had brought it.

"Then let the bird fly away," she said, and she would on no account allow the Prince to come in.

But he was not to be disheartened; he smeared his face with black and brown, drew his cap over his forehead, and knocked at the Palace door. The Emperor opened it.

"Good day, Emperor," he said. "Could I get work at the Palace?"

"Well, there are so many wanting places," said the Emperor; "but let me see!—I need a Swineherd. I have a good many pigs to keep."

So the Prince was made Imperial Swineherd. He had a wretched little room near the pig-sty and here he was obliged to stay. But the whole day he sat and worked, and by the evening he had made a neat little pipkin, and round it was a set of bells, and as soon as the pot began to boil, the bells fell to jingling most sweetly and played the old melody:

"Ach du lieber Augustin,
Alles ist weg, weg, weg!" [1]

---

[1] Alas! dear Augustin,
All is lost, lost, lost!

But the most wonderful thing was that when you held your finger in the steam of the pipkin, you could immediately smell what dinner was cooking on every hearth in the town. That was something very different from a rose.

The Princess was walking out with her ladies-in-waiting, and when she heard the melody, she stopped short, and looked pleased, for she could play "Ach du lieber Augustin" herself; it was the only tune she knew, and that she played with one finger. "Why, that is the tune I play," she said. "What a cultivated Swineherd he must be. Go down and ask him how much his instrument costs."

So one of the ladies-in-waiting was obliged to go down, but she put on pattens first.

"How much do you want for your pipkin?" asked the Lady-in-waiting.

"I will have ten kisses from the Princess," said the Swineherd.

"Good gracious!" said the Lady-in-waiting.

"I will not take less," said the Swineherd.

"Well, what did he say?" asked the Princess.

"I really cannot tell you," said the Lady-in-waiting. "It is too dreadful."

"Then you must whisper it," said the Princess. So she whispered it.

"He is very rude," said the Princess, and she walked away. But she had gone only a few steps when the bells sounded so sweetly:

"Ach du lieber Augustin,
Alles ist weg, weg, weg!"

"Listen," said the Princess, "ask him whether he will have his kisses from my Ladies-in-waiting."

"No, thank you," said the Swineherd. "I will have ten kisses from the Princess, or, I will keep my pipkin."

"How tiresome!" said the Princess; "but you must stand round me, so that nobody shall see."

So the ladies-in-waiting stood round her, and they spread out their skirts. The Swineherd got the kisses, and she got the pipkin.

How delighted she was. All the evening, and the whole of the next day, that pot was made to boil. And you might have known what everybody was cooking on every hearth in the town, from the Chamberlain's to the shoemaker's. The court ladies danced and clapped their hands.

"We know who is to have fruit-soup and pancakes, and we know who is going to have porridge, and cutlets. How very interesting it is!"

"Most interesting, indeed," said the first Lady-of-Honor.

"Yes, but hold your tongues, for I am the Emperor's daughter."

"Of course we will," they cried in one breath.

The Swineherd, or the Prince, nobody knew that he was not a real Swineherd, did not let the day pass without doing something, and he made a rattle which could play all the waltzes, and the polkas and the hop-dances which had been known since the creation of the world.

"But this is *superbe!*" said the Princess, who was just passing: "I have never heard more beautiful composition. Go and ask him what the instrument costs. But I will give no more kisses."

"He insists on a hundred kisses from the Princess," said the ladies-in-waiting who had been down to ask.

"I think he must be quite mad," said the Princess, and she walked away. But when she had taken a few steps, she stopped short, and said: "One must encourage the fine arts, and I am the Emperor's daughter. Tell him he may have ten kisses, as before, and the rest he can take from my ladies-in-waiting."

"Yes, but we object to that," said the ladies-in-waiting.

"That is nonsense," said the Princess. "If I can kiss him, surely you can do the same. Go down at once. Don't I give you board and wages?"

So the ladies-in-waiting were obliged to go down to the Swineherd again.

"A hundred kisses from the Princess, or each keeps his own."

"Stand round me," she said. And all the ladies-in-waiting stood round her, and the Swineherd began to kiss her.

"What can all that crowd be down by the pigsty?" said the Emperor, stepping out onto the balcony. He rubbed his eyes and put on his spectacles. "It is the court ladies up to some of their tricks. I must go down and look after them." He pulled up his slippers, for they were shoes which he had trodden down at the heel.

Gracious goodness, how he hurried! As soon as he came into the garden, he walked very softly, and the ladies-in-waiting had so much to do counting the kisses, so that everything could be done fairly, and that the Swineherd should get neither too many nor too few, that they never noticed the Emperor at all. He stood on tip-toe.

"What is this all about?" he said, when he saw the kissing that was going on, and he hit them on the head with his slipper, just as the Swineherd was getting the eighty-sixth kiss. "Heraus!" said the Emperor, for he was angry, and both the Princess and the Swineherd were turned out of his Kingdom.

The Princess wept, the Swineherd scolded, and the rain streamed down.

"Oh! wretched creature that I am," said the Princess. "If I had only taken the handsome Prince! Oh, how unhappy I am!"

Then the Swineherd went behind a tree, washed the black and brown off his face, threw off his ragged clothes, and stood forth in his royal apparel, looking so handsome that she was obliged to curtsey.

"I have learned to despise you," he said. "You would not have an honorable Prince. You could not appreciate a rose or a nightingale, but for a musical toy, you kissed the Swineherd. Now you have your reward."

So he went into his Kingdom, shut the door and bolted it, and she had to stand outside singing:

"Ach du lieber Augustin,
Alles ist weg, weg, weg"!

THE NIGHTINGALE

In China, you must know, the Emperor is a Chinaman, and all those around him are Chinamen, too. It is many years since all this happened, and for that very reason it is worth hearing, before it is forgotten.

The Emperor's palace was the most beautiful in the world; built all of fine porcelain and very costly, but so fragile that it was very difficult to touch, and you had to be very careful in doing so. The most wonderful flowers were to be seen in the garden, and to the most beautiful, silver bells, tinkling bells were tied, for fear people should pass by without noticing them. How well everything had been thought out in the Emperor's garden! This was so big, that the gardener himself did not know where it ended. If you walked on and on you came to the most beautiful forest, with tall trees and big lakes. The wood stretched right down to the sea which was blue and deep; great ships could pass underneath the branches, and here a nightingale had made its home, and its singing was so entrancing that the poor fisherman, though he had so many other things to do, would lie still and listen when he was out at night drawing in his nets.

"How beautiful it is!" he said; but then he was forced to think about his own affairs, and the Nightingale was forgotten. The next day, when it sang again, the fisherman said the same thing: "How beautiful it is!"

Travellers from all the countries of the world came to the Emperor's town, and expressed their admiration of the palace and the garden, but when they heard the Nightingale, they all said: "This is the best of all!"

Now, when these travellers came home, they told of what they had seen. And scholars wrote many books about the town, the palace and the garden, but nobody left out the Nightingale; it was always spoken of as the most wonderful of all they had seen. And those who had the gift of the Poet, wrote the most delightful poems all about the Nightingale in the wood near the deep lake.

The books went round the world, and in the course of time some of them reached the Emperor. He sat in his golden chair, and read and read, nodding his head every minute; for it pleased him to read the beautiful descriptions of the town, the palace and the garden.

"But the Nightingale is the best of all," he read.

"What is this?" said the Emperor. "The Nightingale! I know nothing whatever about it. To think of there being such a bird in my Kingdom—nay in my very garden—and I have never heard it. And to think one should learn such a thing for the first time from a book!"

Then he summoned his Lord in Waiting, who was such a grand personage that if anyone inferior in rank ventured to speak to him, or ask him about anything, he merely answered "P," which meant nothing whatever.

"There is said to be a most wonderful bird, called the Nightingale," said the Emperor; "they say it is the best thing in my great Kingdom. Why have I been told nothing about it?"

"I have never heard it mentioned before," said the Lord-in-Waiting. "It has certainly never been presented at court."

"It is my good pleasure that it shall appear tonight and sing before me!" said the Emperor. "The whole world knows what is mine, and I myself do not know it."

"I have never heard it mentioned before," said the Lord-in-Waiting. "I will seek it, and I shall find it."

But where was it to be found? The Lord-in-Waiting ran up and down all the stairs, through the halls and passages, but not one of all those whom he met had ever heard a word about the Nightingale; so the Lord-in-Waiting ran back to the Emperor and told him that it must certainly be a fable invented by writers of books.

"Your Majesty must not believe all that is written in books. It is pure invention, something which is called the Black Art."

"But," said the Emperor, "the book in which I have read this was sent to me by His Majesty, the Emperor of Japan, and therefore this cannot be a falsehood. I *will* hear the Nightingale. It must appear this evening! It has my Imperial favor, and if it fails to appear the Court shall be trampled upon after the Court has supped."

"Tsing-pe!" said the Lord-in-Waiting, and again he ran up and down all the stairs, through all the halls and passages, and half the Court ran with him, for they had no wish to be trampled upon. And many questions were asked about the wonderful Nightingale, of whom all had heard except those who lived at Court.

At last, they met a poor little girl in the kitchen. She said: "Oh, yes! The Nightingale! I know it well. How it can sing! Every evening I have permission to take the broken pieces from the table to my poor sick mother who lives near the seashore, and on my way back, when I feel tired, and rest a while in the wood, then I hear the Nightingale sing, and my eyes are filled with tears; it is as if my mother kissed me."

"Little kitchen-maid," said the Lord-in-Waiting, "I will get a permanent place for you in the Court Kitchen and permission to see the Emperor dine, if you can lead us to the Nightingale; for it has been commanded to appear at Court to-night."

So they started off all together where the bird used to sing; half the Court went, too. They were going along at a good pace, when suddenly they heard a cow lowing.

"Oh," said a Court-Page. "There it is! What wonderful power for so small a creature! I have certainly heard it before."

"No, those are the cows lowing," said the little kitchen-maid. "We are a long way from the place yet."

Then the frogs began to croak in the marsh. "Glorious," said the Court-Preacher. "Now, I hear it—it is just like little church-bells."

"No, those are the frogs," said the little kitchen-maid. "But now I think we shall soon hear it."

And then the Nightingale began to sing.

"There it is," said the little girl. "Listen, listen—there it sits!" And she pointed to a little gray bird in the branches.

"Is it possible!" said the Lord-in-Waiting. "I had never supposed it would look like that. How very plain it looks! It has certainly lost its color from seeing so many grand folk here."

"Little Nightingale," called out the little kitchen-maid, "our gracious Emperor wishes you to sing for him."

"With the greatest pleasure," said the Nightingale, and it sang, and it was a joy to hear it.

"It sounds like little glass bells," said the Lord-in-Waiting; "and just look at its little throat, how it moves! It is astonishing to think we have never heard it before! It will have a real *succes* at Court."

"Shall I sing for the Emperor again?" asked the Nightingale, who thought that the Emperor was there in person.

"Mine excellent little Nightingale," said the Lord-in-Waiting, "I have the great pleasure of bidding you to a Court-Festival this night, when you will enchant His Imperial Majesty with your delightful warbling."

"My voice sounds better among the green trees," said the Nightingale. But it came willingly when it knew that the Emperor wished it.

There was a great deal of furbishing up at the palace. The walls and ceiling which were of porcelain, shone with the light of a thousand golden lamps. The most beautiful flowers of the tinkling kind were placed in the passages. There was a running to and fro and a great draught, but that is just what made the bells ring, and one could not hear oneself speak. In the middle of the great hall where the Emperor sat, a golden rod had been set up on which the Nightingale was to perch. The whole Court was present, and the little kitchen-maid was allowed to stand behind the door, for she had now the actual title of Court Kitchen-Maid. All were there in their smartest clothes, and they all looked toward the little gray bird to which the Emperor nodded.

And then the Nightingale sang, so gloriously that tears sprang into the Emperor's eyes and rolled down his cheeks, and the Nightingale sang even more sweetly. The song went straight to the heart, and the Emperor was so delighted that he declared that the Nightingale should have his golden slipper to hang round its neck. But the Nightingale declined. It had already had its reward.

"I have seen tears in the Emperor's eyes. That is my greatest reward. An Emperor's tears have a wonderful power. God knows I am sufficiently rewarded," and again its sweet, glorious voice was heard.

"That is the most delightful coquetting I have ever known," said the ladies sitting round, and they took water into their mouths, in order to gurgle when anyone spoke to them, and they really thought they were like the Nightingale. Even the footmen and the chambermaids sent word that they were satisfied, and that means a great deal, for they are always the most difficult people to please. Yes, indeed, there was no doubt as to the Nightingale's success. It was to stay at Court, and have its own cage, with liberty to go out twice in the daytime, and once at night. Twelve footmen went out with it, and each held a silk ribbon which was tied to the bird's leg, and which they held very tightly. There was not much pleasure in an outing of that sort. The whole town was talking about the wonderful bird, and when two people met, one said: "Nightin——" and the other said "gale," and they sighed and understood one another. Eleven cheesemongers' children were called after the bird, though none of them could sing a note.

One day a large parcel came for the Emperor. Outside was written the word: "Nightingale."

"Here we have a new book about our wonderful bird," said the Emperor. But it was not a book; it was a little work of art which lay in a box—an artificial Nightingale, which looked exactly like the real one, but it was studded all over with diamonds, rubies and sapphires. As soon as you wound it up, it could sing one of the songs which the real bird sang, and its tail moved up and down and glittered with silver and gold. Round its neck was a ribbon on which was written: "The Emperor of Japan's Nightingale is poor indeed, compared with the Emperor of China's."

"That is delightful," they all said, and on the messenger who had brought the artificial bird, they bestowed the title of "Imperial Nightingale-Bringer-in-Chief."

"Let them sing together, and *what* a duet that will be!"

And so they had to sing, but the thing would not work, because the real Nightingale could only sing in its own way, and the artificial Nightingale went by clockwork.

"That is not its fault," said the band-master. "Time is its strong point and it has quite my method."

Then the artificial Nightingale had to sing alone. It had just as much success as the real bird, and it was so much handsomer to look at; it glittered like bracelets and breast-pins. It sang the same tune three and thirty times, and still it was not tired; the people would willingly listen to the whole performance over again from the start, but the Emperor suggested that the real Nightingale should sing for a while—where was it? Nobody had noticed it had flown out of the open window back to its green woods.

"But what is the meaning of all this?" said the Emperor. All the courtiers railed at the Nightingale and said it was a most ungrateful creature.

"We have the better of the two," they said, and the artificial Nightingale had to sing again, and this was the thirty-fourth time they had heard the same tune. But they did not know it properly even then, because it was so difficult, and the band-master praised the wonderful bird in the highest terms and even asserted that it was superior to the real bird, not only as regarded the outside, with the many lovely diamonds, but the inside as well.

"You see, ladies and gentlemen, and above all your Imperial Majesty, that with the real Nightingale, you can never predict what may happen, but with the artificial bird, everything is settled beforehand; so it remains and it cannot be changed. One can account for it. One can rip it open, and show the human ingenuity, explaining how the cylinders lie, how they work, and how one thing is the result of another."

"That is just what we think," they all exclaimed, and the band-master received permission to exhibit the bird to the people on the following Sunday. The Emperor said they would hear it sing. They listened, and were as much delighted as if they had been drunk with tea, which is Chinese, you know, and they all said: "Oh!" and stuck their forefingers in the air, and nodded their heads. But the poor fisherman who had heard the real Nightingale, said: "It sounds quite well, and a little like it, but there is something wanting, I do not know what."

The real Nightingale was banished from the Kingdom.

The artificial bird had its place on a silken cushion close to the Emperor's bed. All the presents it had received, the gold and precious stones, lay all round it, and it had been honored with the title of High-Imperial-Bed-Room-Singer—in the first rank, on the left side, for even the Emperor considered that side the grander on which the heart is placed, and even an Emperor has his heart on the left side.

The band-master wrote twenty-five volumes about the wonderful artificial bird. The book was very learned and very long, filled with the most difficult words in the Chinese language, and everybody said they had read and understood it, for otherwise they would have been considered stupid, and would have been trampled upon.

And thus a whole year passed away. The Emperor, the Court, and all the Chinamen knew every little gurgle in the artificial bird's song, and just for this reason, they were all the better pleased with it. They could sing it themselves—which they did.

The boys in the street sang "Zi-zi-zi," and "cluck, cluck," and even the Emperor sang it. Yes, it was certainly beautiful!

But one evening, while the bird was singing, and the Emperor lay in bed listening to it, there was a whirring sound inside the bird, and something whizzed; all the wheels ran round, and the music stopped.

The Emperor sprang out of bed and sent for the Court Physician, but what could he do? Then they sent for the watch-maker, and after much talk and examination, he patched the bird up, but he said it must be spared as much as possible, because the hammers were so worn out—and he could not put new ones in so that the music could be counted on. This was a great grief. The bird could only be allowed to sing once a year, and even that was risky, but on these occasions, the band-master would make a little speech, full of difficult words, saying the bird was just as good as ever—and that was true.

Five years passed away, and a great sorrow had come to the country. The people all really cared for their Emperor, and now he was ill and it was said he could not live. A new Emperor had been chosen, and the people stood about the streets, and questioned the Lord-in-Waiting about their Emperor's condition.

"P!" he said, and shook his head.

The Emperor lay pale and cold on his great, gorgeous bed; the whole Court believed that he was dead, and they all hastened to pay homage to the new Emperor. The footmen hurried off to discuss matters, and the chambermaids gave a great coffee-party. Cloth had been laid down in all the rooms and passages, so that not a footstep should be heard and it was all so very quiet. But the Emperor was not yet dead. He lay stiff and pale in the sumptuous bed, with its long velvet curtains and heavy gold tassels; high above was an open window, and the moon shone in upon the Emperor and the artificial bird. The poor Emperor could hardly breathe; he felt as if someone were sitting on his chest; he opened his eyes and saw that it was Death sitting on his chest, wearing his golden crown, holding in one hand his golden sword, and in the other his splendid banner. And from the folds of the velvet curtains strange faces peered forth; some terrible to look on, others mild and friendly—these were the Emperor's good and bad deeds, which gazed upon him now that Death sat upon his heart.

"Do you remember this?" whispered one after the other. "Do you remember that?" They told him so much that the sweat poured down his face.

"I never knew that," said the Emperor. "Music! music! Beat the great Chinese drum!" he called out, "so that I may not hear what they are saying!"

But they kept on, and Death nodded his head, like a Chinaman, at everything they said.

"Music, music," cried the Emperor. "You precious little golden bird! Sing to me, ah! sing to me! I have given you gold and costly treasures. I have hung my golden slipper about your neck. Sing to me. Sing to me!"

But the bird was silent; there was no one to wind him up, and therefore he could not sing.

Death went on, staring at the Emperor with his great hollow eyes, and it was terribly still.

Then, suddenly, close to the window, came the sound of a lovely song. It was the little live Nightingale perched on a branch outside. It had heard of its Emperor's need, and had therefore flown hither to bring him comfort and hope, and as he sang, the faces became paler and the blood coursed more freely through the Emperor's veins. Even Death himself listened and said: "Go on, little Nightingale. Go on."

"Yes, if you will give me the splendid sword. Yes, if you will give me the Imperial banner! Yes, if you will give me the Emperor's crown!"

And Death gave back all these treasures for a song. And still the Nightingale sang on. He sang of the quiet churchyard, where the white roses grow, where the elder flowers bloom, and where the grass is kept moist by the tears of those left behind, and there came to Death such a longing to see his garden, that he floated out of the window, like a cold white mist.

"Thank you, thank you," said the Emperor. "You heavenly little bird, I know you well! I banished you from the land, and you have charmed away the evil spirits from my bed and you have driven Death from my heart. How shall I reward you?"

"You have rewarded me," said the Nightingale.

"I brought tears to your eyes the first time I sang, and I shall never forget that. Those are the jewels which touched the heart of the singer; but sleep now, that you may wake fresh and strong. I will sing to you." Then it sang again, and the Emperor fell into a sweet sleep.

The sun shone in upon him through the window, when he woke the next morning feeling strong and well. None of his servants had come back, because they thought he was dead, but the Nightingale was still singing.

"You will always stay with me," said the Emperor. "You shall only sing when it pleases you, and I will break the artificial Nightingale into a thousand pieces."

"Do not do that," said the Nightingale. "It has done the best it could. Keep it with you. I cannot build my nest in a palace, but let me come just as I please. I will sit on the branch near the window, and sing to you that you may be both joyful and thoughtful. I will sing to you of the happy folk, and of those that suffer; I will sing of the evil and of the good, which is being hidden from you. The little singing bird flies hither and thither, to the poor fisherman, to the peasant's hut, to many who live far from you and the Court. Your heart is dearer to me than your crown, and yet the crown has a breath of sanctity, too. I will come, I will sing to you! But one thing you must promise me!"

"All that you ask," said the Emperor, and stood there in his imperial robes which he had put on himself, and held the heavy golden sword on his heart.

"I beg you, let no one know that you have a little bird who tells you everything. It will be far better so!"

Then the Nightingale flew away.

The servants came to look upon their dead Emperor. Yes, there they stood; and the Emperor said: "Good morning!"

THE PRINCESS ON THE PEA

There was once a Prince who wished to marry a Princess, but she must be a *real* Princess. He travelled all over the world to find one, but there was always something wrong. There were plenty of Princesses, but whether they were *real* or not he could not be sure. There was always something that was not quite right. So he came home again, feeling very sad, for he was so anxious to have a real Princess.

One evening there was a terrible storm; it lightened and thundered, and the rain came down in torrents; it was a fearful night. In the midst of the storm there came a knocking at the town-gate, and the old King himself went down to open it. There, outside, stood a Princess. But what a state she was in from the rain and the storm! The water was running out of her hair on to her clothes, into her shoes and out at the heels; and yet she said she was a *real* Princess.

"We shall soon find out about that," thought the old Queen. But she said never a word. She went into the bedroom, took off all the bedclothes and put a pea on the bedstead. Then she took twenty mattresses and laid them on the pea and twenty eider-down quilts on the mattresses. And the Princess was to sleep on the top of all.

In the morning they came to her and asked her how she had slept.

"Oh! wretchedly," said the Princess. "I scarcely closed my eyes the whole night long. Heaven knows what could have been in the bed! I have lain upon something hard, so that my whole body is black and blue. It is quite dreadful."

They could see now that she was a *real* Princess, because she had felt the pea through twenty mattresses and twenty eider-down quilts. Nobody but a real Princess could be so sensitive.

So the Prince married her, for now he knew that he had found a *real* Princess, and the pea was sent to an Art Museum, where it can still be seen, if nobody has taken it away.

Now, mark you: This is a true story.

PART III

A NEW LIST OF STORIES

Compiled by

Eulalie Steinmetz

SUPERVISOR OF STORYTELLING
THE NEW YORK PUBLIC LIBRARY

NOTE

For thirty-six years Miss Shedlock's book has been the touchstone to the art of storytelling. Various forces and circumstances have influenced the choice of titles for this list of stories to accompany its third edition: the obligation to make the list reflect Miss Shedlock's own interest and high standards, the need to provide material for both the beginning storyteller and the experienced one, and the necessity of reminding storytellers and publishers of the many storytelling books which are out of print.

This is a selective list intended as an invitation to the storyteller to read and search and discover on his own.

1951

EULALIE STEINMETZ

FANCIFUL STORIES

THE APPLE OF CONTENTMENT. In: *Pepper and Salt,* by Howard Pyle. Harper. (Dover reprint.)

One could list all the stories in *Pepper and Salt* for the storyteller, so perfectly are they suited to his art.

THE CAT THAT WALKED BY HIMSELF. In: *Just So Stories,* by Rudyard Kipling. Doubleday.

This and "The Butterfly that Stamped" are the more sophisticated of the *Just So Stories,* and the most difficult to tell.

THE CHINESE FAIRY-TALE. In: *Moonshine and Clover,* by Laurence Housman. Harcourt, Brace. o.p.

The story of an artist's genius, one which Miss Shedlock recreated for American audiences with sensitivity and understanding. It can also be found in Mary Gould Davis's *A Baker's Dozen* (Harcourt, Brace).

THE ELEPHANT'S CHILD. In: *Just So Stories,* by Rudyard Kipling. Doubleday.

Both the plot and the words of this perfectly constructed story are enjoyed by the younger children. They also like "How the Whale Got His Throat" and "How the Rhinoceros Got His Skin."

ELSIE PIDDOCK SKIPS IN HER SLEEP. In: *Martin Pippin in the Daisy-Field,* by Eleanor Farjeon. Lippincott.

A story for Spring, as pleasing to all girls, big and little, as is "The Little Dressmaker" in the author's *One Foot in Fairyland* (Lippincott. o.p.).

THE GREAT QUILLOW, by James Thurber. Harcourt, Brace.

A story that is at once simple, sophisticated and contemporary.

THE KING OF TRIPOLI BRINGS THE PASTA. In: *Italian Peepshow,* by Eleanor Farjeon. Lippincott. o.p.

It is to be regretted that only through the storyteller's art can the fresh plots and distinctive writing of these stories be brought to the children.

THE LIGHT PRINCESS, by George MacDonald. Illustrated by Dorothy Lathrop. Macmillan.

When cut for telling this story of a princess who lost her gravity is an appealing and dramatic one.

THE LOST HALF-HOUR. In: *The Firelight Fairy Book,* by Henry Beston. Little, Brown. o.p.

A completely satisfying story of wonder and magic. "The Seller of Dreams" is a modern fairy tale, shorter and easier to tell.

THE LOVELY MYFANWY. In: *Broomsticks and Other Tales,* by Walter de la Mare. Knopf.

The delicate humor in this romantic story appeals to older girls.

MR. MURDLE'S LARGE HEART. In: *A Street of Little Shops,* by Margery Williams Bianco. Doubleday.

An original story for Saint Valentine's Day distinguished for its humor and keen observation of the American small-town scene. "The Baker's Daughter" is a good choice for a birthday celebration.

MY GRANDFATHER, HENDRY WATTY, by Arthur Quiller-Couch. In: *Twenty-Four Unusual Stories,* by Anna Cogswell Tyler. Harcourt, Brace.

A NEW LIST OF STORIES

A shivery droll for Halloween. This collection of stories is especially valuable to the storyteller because it derives from the storytelling experiences of Miss Tyler.

THE PINK GERANIUM. In: *Long Ago in Rouen,* by Ida Withers. Oxford University Press.

Gallic whimsy at its best. "A Silly Story" and "Monsieur Corneille's Crumple-Dumplet" are equally light and gay.

THE PIPER AT THE GATES OF DAWN. In: *The Wind in the Willows,* by Kenneth Grahame. Scribner.

If this chapter is to introduce Kenneth Grahame to the children, it must be given to them in his own memorable words. "Dulce Domum" is for the Christmas storyhour.

PRINCESS FINOLA AND THE DWARF. In: *The Golden Spears,* by Edmund Leamy. Longmans, Green. o.p.

There is faerie atmosphere in these stories of Old Ireland.

THE RAT-CATCHER'S DAUGHTER. In: *A Doorway in Fairyland,* by Laurence Housman. Harcourt, Brace. o.p.

This is the easiest to tell of the Housman fairy tales but "The Traveller's Shoes" is also well spun, and "The Wooing of the Maze" has an unexpected denouement.

RIDDLES IN THE DARK. In: *The Hobbit,* by J. R. R. Tolkien. Houghton Mifflin.

Bilbo and Gollum's riddle contest makes a good Halloween story and introduces an original fantasy to the children.

"RIKKI-TIKKI-TAVI." In: *The Jungle Book,* by Rudyard Kipling. Doubleday.

The heroic story of the mongoose who has become one of the outstanding characters in modern literature.

THE SELFISH GIANT. In: *The Happy Prince and Other Fairy Tales,* by Oscar Wilde. Putnam.

A miracle story for Easter, more easily told than "The Happy Prince" or the poignant "The Birthday of the Infanta."

THE SILVER HEN. In: *The Pot of Gold,* by Mary E. Wilkins. Lothrop. o.p.

This and "The Christmas Masquerade" provide two stories for the holiday season that are sound in plot and unknown to most children. For the same reasons "The Pumpkin Giant" is good for Halloween or Thanksgiving.

THE SWAN MAIDEN. In: *The Wonder Clock,* by Howard Pyle. Harper. (Dover reprint.)

With only *The Wonder Clock* to draw upon, a storyteller could face triumphantly any audience: large or small, old or young, naive or sophisticated.

THE TAILOR OF GLOUCESTER, by Beatrix Potter. Warne.

All of Beatrix Potter's tightly-knit stories make excellent material for the storyhour.

THE TOYS. In: *The Treasure of Li-Po,* by Alice Ritchie. Harcourt, Brace.

The breath of Old China is in this well-written story of a small girl who wanted to be a sailor. "Two of Everything" has the wisdom and the pattern of a folk tale.

THE VELVETEEN RABBIT; OR, HOW TOYS BECOME REAL, by Margery Williams Bianco. Doubleday.

A Christmas story for the little children with William Nicholson's interpretive illustrations.

THE WHITE HORSE GIRL AND THE BLUE WIND BOY. In: *Rootabaga Stories,* by Carl Sandburg. Omnibus volume. Harcourt, Brace.

Carl Sandburg's love for America finds poetical expression in this allegory for older boys and girls.

HANS CHRISTIAN ANDERSEN

A careful reading and comparison of the editions and translations of an Andersen story are prerequisites before deciding which version to present at the storyhour.

THE EMPEROR'S NEW CLOTHES. In: *Andersen's Fairy Tales.* Illustrated by Elizabeth MacKinstry. With an introduction by Anne Carroll Moore. Coward-McCann.

Miss MacKinstry selected the text for her book from the Author's Edition of *Wonder Stories* and *Stories and Tales,* illustrated by Lieutenant V. Pedersen and M. L. Stone and published by Houghton Mifflin.

THE FIR-TREE. In: *Fairy Tales and Legends,* by Hans Andersen. Illustrated by Rex Whistler. London. The Bodley Head.

The text of the Rex Whistler Andersen is based in part on the translation of Mrs. Lucas and in part on that of Caroline Peachey.

HANS CLODHOPPER. In: *Fairy Tales from Hans Christian Andersen.* Translated by Mrs. E. Lucas. Dutton. o.p.

IT'S PERFECTLY TRUE! In: *It's Perfectly True and Other Stories,* by Hans Christian Andersen. Translated from the Danish by Paul Leyssac. Harcourt, Brace.

THE NIGHTINGALE. In: *The Art of the Story-Teller,* by Marie L. Shedlock. Dover Publications, Inc.

In telling Andersen Miss Shedlock used chiefly *Fairy Tales and Other Stories,* by Hans Christian Andersen, revised and in part newly translated by W. A. and J. K. Craigie and published by the Oxford University Press.

THE PRINCESS ON THE PEA. In: *The Art of the Story-Teller,* by Marie L. Shedlock. Dover Publications, Inc.

THE STEADFAST TIN SOLDIER. In: *Andersen's Fairy Tales.* Illustrated by Elizabeth MacKinstry. With an introduction by Anne Carroll Moore. Coward-McCann.

THE SWINEHERD. In: *The Art of the Story-Teller,* by Marie L. Shedlock. Dover Publications, Inc.

"THUMBELISA." In: *Fairy Tales from Hans Christian Andersen.* Translated by Mrs. E. Lucas. Dutton. o.p.

THE TINDER BOX. In: *Forty Stories,* by Hans Andersen. Newly translated from the Danish by M. R. James. Lippincott. o.p.

THE UGLY DUCKLING. In: *Fairy Tales and Legends,* by Hans Andersen. Illustrated by Rex Whistler. London. The Bodley Head.

THE WILD SWANS. In: *Wonder Stories Told for Children,* by Hans Christian Andersen. Author's Edition. Houghton Mifflin.

A NEW LIST OF STORIES

POETRY AND NONSENSE

COME HITHER; A COLLECTION OF RHYMES AND POEMS FOR THE YOUNG OF ALL AGES. Made by Walter de la Mare. Knopf.

A selection of poetry in which the poet-compiler reveals the distinction of his own spirit and mind.

THE COMPLETE NONSENSE BOOK, by Edward Lear. Faber & Faber, Ltd. (Dover reprint.)

The storyteller is reminded of Miss Shedlock's advice: "One might occasionally introduce into the storyhour one of Edward Lear's 'Nonsense Rhymes.'"

HOW CATS CAME TO PURR. In: *The Pigtail of Ah Lee Ben Loo,* by John Bennett. Longmans, Green. o.p.

Sooty Will's misadventures with a coffee-mill. This story is also in Mary Noel Bleecker's *Big Music* (Viking).

HOW THE ARISTOCRATS SAILED AWAY. In: *The Reformed Pirate,* by Frank Stockton. Scribner.

Grave absurdity that given the right storyteller, is irresistible.

A MAD TEA-PARTY. In: *Alice's Adventures in Wonderland,* by Lewis Carroll. With forty-two illustrations by John Tenniel. Macmillan.

Every storyteller will have his own favorite chapter of *Alice* to share with the children on Lewis Carroll's birthday on January 27th.

THE MAGIC FISHBONE, by Charles Dickens. Warne.

F. D. Bedford's jolly pictures extend the gay and festive spirit of this Christmas classic.

THE PALACE ON THE ROCK. In: *Don't Blame Me!* by Richard Hughes. Harper. o.p.

Fantastically logical nonsense characterizes these stories and those in the author's *The Spider's Palace* (Harper. o.p.). In the latter title "Living in W'ales" and "The Dark Child" are good fun to tell.

A POCKETFUL OF RHYMES, edited by Katherine Love. Crowell.

Miss Love used these verses with the children in her own story-hours.

A ROCKET IN MY POCKET, compiled by Carl Withers. Holt.

"Rhymes, chants, game songs, tongue twisters and ear-teasers" to enliven any storyhour.

THE WEDDING PROCESSION OF THE RAG DOLL AND THE BROOM HANDLE AND WHO WAS IN IT. In: *Rootabaga Stories,* by Carl Sandburg. Omnibus volume. Harcourt, Brace.

The droll nonsense of this and "Shush Shush, the Big Buff Banty Hen Who Laid an Egg in the Postmaster's Hat" makes them favorite stories with the younger children.

STORIES OF SAINTS

THE CONVERSION OF ST. WILFRID. In: *Rewards and Fairies,* by Rudyard Kipling. Doubleday.

A dramatic story of the early days of Christianity in Britain.

THE FIRST CHRISTMAS CRIB, by Katherine Milhous. Scribner.

Saint Francis of Assisi made the crêche for an Umbrian village church.

A NEW LIST OF STORIES

JOAN OF ARC, by M. Boutet de Monvel. Appleton-Century. o.p.

The classic presentation of the French Saint for American children.

THE LEGEND OF SAINT ELIZABETH. In: *The Way of the Storyteller,* by Ruth Sawyer. Viking.

The first miracle wrought by the patron Saint of Hungary.

THE PEDDLER OF BALLAGHADEREEN. In: *The Way of the Storyteller,* by Ruth Sawyer. Viking.

An Irish folk tale about Saint Patrick. Eleanor Farjeon has a dramatic and heroic version of the Saint's life in her *Ten Saints* (Oxford University Press).

SAINT CHRISTOPHER. In: *Ten Saints,* by Eleanor Farjeon. Oxford University Press.

The familiar legend of Saint Christopher carrying the Christ Child through the waters supplements the version given in *The Art of the Story-Teller.*

ST. CIARAN AND BROTHER FOX AND BROTHER BADGER. In: *Beasts and Saints,* by Helen Waddell. London. Constable and Company.

Stories of simple faith translated "without sophistication" from Latin sources. The legends about the gentle Saint Jerome and the Irish Saint Kevin are also good for storytelling.

SAINT MARTIN AND THE HONEST MAN. In: *The Forge in the Forest,* by Padraic Colum. Macmillan. o.p.

How Saint Martin, in the guise of a white horse, roams the earth each All Saints' Day seeking an honest man.

SAINT NICHOLAS' TRAVELS, by Hertha Pauli. Houghton Mifflin. o.p.

A good explanation of the Saint Nicholas-Santa Claus legend to use with the chapter about the Saint in Eleanor Farjeon's *Ten Saints* (Oxford University Press).

THE STORY OF GOOD SAINT ANNE. In: *Thunder in the Mountains,* by H. M. Hooke. Oxford University Press.

A Canadian legend about the founding of the shrine of Saint Anne de Beaupré.

THE TRUCE OF THE WOLF. In: *The Truce of the Wolf and Other Tales of Old Italy,* by Mary Gould Davis. Harcourt, Brace. o.p.

In preparing to tell the story of Saint Francis of Assisi and the Wolf of Gubbio read *The Seven Miracles of Gubbio* by R. L. Bruckberger (Whittlesey House). Both Miss Davis and Mr. Bruckberger base their versions on the *Fioretti* of Saint Francis.

MYTH AND LEGEND

The telling of a hero tale presupposes a wide knowledge of source material and a thorough understanding of the hero and his times. The versions given here are best for the story-hour but all of them require cutting and adapting before oral interpretation.

ORPHEUS WITH HIS LUTE, by W. M. Hutchinson. Longmans, Green.

The telling of any Greek myth is enriched by the reading of this book.

CUPID AND PSYCHE. In: *A Book of Myths,* with illustrations by Helen Sewell. Macmillan.

A good introduction to Greek mythology because its motifs are familiar to children through the folk tale.

A NEW LIST OF STORIES

PROMETHEUS THE FIREBRINGER. In: *Orpheus with His Lute,* by W. M. Hutchinson. Longmans, Green.

A clear, metrical version which includes the story of Pandora.

THE CURSE OF ECHO, by Elsie Finnimore Buckley. In: *Twenty-Four Unusual Stories,* by Anna Cogswell Tyler. Harcourt, Brace.

A flower legend to tell when the narcissi are in blossom.

THE MOTHER AND THE MAID. In: *Orpheus with His Lute,* by W. M. Hutchinson. Longmans, Green.

The Ceres-Proserpina myth is called "The Pomegranate Seeds" in Nathaniel Hawthorne's *Tanglewood Tales* (Houghton Mifflin).

PHAETON. In: *The Forge in the Forest,* by Padraic Colum. Macmillan. o.p.

"Young Phaeton fell from his father's chariot, but even so he lost nothing of his glory, for his heart was set upon the doing of great things." "Bellerophon" — the story of Pegasus, the winged horse — is a good companion story.

THE ADVENTURES OF ODYSSEUS AND THE TALE OF TROY, by Padraic Colum. Macmillan.

Padraic Colum, a storyteller himself, gives the clearest versions for cycle storytelling of the episodic adventures of the Greek heroes.

THE QUEST OF THE HAMMER. In: *In the Days of Giants,* by Abbie Farwell Brown. Houghton Mifflin.

A broadly humorous episode from the Icelandic Edda which appeals to older boys and girls.

BALDER AND THE MISTLETOE. In: *In the Days of Giants,* by Abbie Farwell Brown. Houghton Mifflin.

Gudrun Thorne-Thomsen has made a recording of this Norse story for the American Library Association.

VAINAMOINEN. In: *Heroes of the Kalevala,* by Babette Deutsch. Messner.

For the cycle telling of the Kalevala use its four heroes — Vainamoinen, Ilmarinen, Kullervo and Lemminkainen — as the basis for division and concentration of action.

BY HIS OWN MIGHT, by Dorothy Hosford. Holt.

The Anglo-Saxon epic can be told to children as a trilogy, the climax of each story being one of the battles of Beowulf.

THE STORY OF ROLAND, by James Baldwin. Scribner.

A version of the *Chanson* drawn from many sources and easily adapted for storytelling because of its continuity, detail and delineation of character.

THE STORY OF SIEGFRIED, by James Baldwin. Scribner. o.p.

Three chapters — "The Curse of Gold," "Mimer, the Master" and "Fafnir, the Dragon" — make a trilogy of the Siegfried saga for the storyhour.

THE WINNING OF KINGHOOD. In: *The Story of King Arthur and His Knights,* by Howard Pyle. Scribner. (Dover reprint.)

How Arthur entered his birthright of royalty by drawing the sword from the stone is the proper introduction to the whole cycle of Round Table stories.

HOW THE HARP CAME TO TARA. In: *The Frenzied Prince,* by Padraic Colum. McKay.

An episode from Ireland's Southern epic which tells how Finn MacCuhal became Lord of the *Fianna* at the High Court of Ireland.

THE TANGLE-COATED HORSE. In: *The Tangle-Coated Horse,* by Ella Young. Longmans, Green.

The *Fianna* in one of their more boisterous adventures. Ella Young tells these legends with the imagination of a poet and the art of a storyteller.

HOW CUCHULAIN WOOED HIS WIFE. In: *Cuchulain, the Hound of Ulster,* by Eleanor Hull. Crowell. o.p.

The Ultonian epic can be introduced to older girls by means of this romantic interlude. "The Fight of Cuchulain with His Son Conla" is the Irish parallel of an equally tragic episode in the Persian epic *Sohrab and Rustam.*

SOHRAB AND RUSTAM. In: *Rustam Lion of Persia,* by Alan Lake Chidsey. Minton, Balch. o.p.

Both this version of a "tale replete with tears" and Helen Zimmern's in *The Epic of Kings* (Macmillan. o.p.) are taken from Firdausi's *Shah Naman* the epic of Persia.

THE BENDING OF THE BOW. In: *Rama, Hero of India,* by Dhan Gopal Mukerji. Dutton.

If this source is used to present the *Ramayana* to the children, care must be taken to preserve the oriental richness of Mr. Mukerji's wording. "Half a God and All a Hero" in Mabel A. Beling's *The Wicked Goldsmith* (Harper. o.p.) is a simple yet dramatic retelling of the Hindu epic.

WINABOJO: MASTER OF LIFE, by James Cloyd Bowman. Whitman.

This Indian hero is the original of Longfellow's Hiawatha. The most satisfactory episode for storytelling is the meeting of Winabojo with his father: the Father-of-all-the-Winds, Keeper-of-the-West.

THE BOX OF DAYLIGHT, by William Hurd Hillyer. Knopf. o.p.

The eerie adventures of Raven, an Alaskan Indian hero, in "The Land of the Air" are the easiest to adapt for storytelling.

THE ART OF THE STORY-TELLER

THE FOLK TALE

AH TCHA THE SLEEPER. In: *Shen of the Sea,* by A. B Chrisman. Dutton.

How tea was discovered in China. "Chop-Sticks" is another amusing origin story.

APPLE-TREE WITCH. In: *The Magic Bird of Chomo-Lung-Ma,* by Sybille Noel. Doubleday. o.p.

A strange and remote atmosphere makes this Himalayan witch story a unique one.

BANYAN. In: *Twenty Jataka Tales,* by Noor Inayat. McKay.

A moving story of the rebirth of the Buddha as a king deer. In "The Monkey-Bridge" he is a "monkey amid the monkeys . . . their chief and their guide."

BILLY BEG AND THE BULL. In: *In Chimney Corners,* by Seumas MacManus. Doubleday. o.p.

Seumus MacManus is a storyteller in the great tradition of the Irish shanachy and his folk tales, full of the rhythm and cadence of the speaking voice, lend themselves naturally and easily to oral interpretation.

BLACK MAGIC. In: *Three Golden Oranges,* by R. S. Boggs and M. G. Davis. Longmans, Green.

Since these Spanish folk tales were gathered from storytellers by a storyteller, every one of them is eminently tellable.

THE BOY WHO DREW CATS. In: *Japanese Fairy Tales,* by Lafcadio Hearn. Liveright.

An unusual story for the Halloween storyhour.

A NEW LIST OF STORIES

THE BUDDHA (TO BE) AS TREE-SPIRIT. In: *Eastern Stories and Legends,* by Marie Shedlock. Dutton. o.p.

In her versions of the Buddha rebirth stories, Miss Shedlock has preserved completely the spirit of the originals.

THE CAT AND THE PARROT. In: *How to Tell Stories to Children,* by Sara Cone Bryant. Houghton Mifflin. o.p.

A folk tale from India notable for its extravagant nonsense and cumulative pattern.

CINDERELLA AND THE GLASS SLIPPER. In: *Told Again,* by Walter de la Mare. Knopf.

Walter de la Mare transmutes the French fairy tale into a romance set in a medieval city on a snowy Christmas day.

THE CONCEITED ELEPHANT AND THE VERY LIVELY MOSQUITO. In: *The Folk Tales of a Savage,* by Lobagola. Knopf. o.p.

A West African folk tale in which a mosquito vanquishes an elephant. It is also in Mary Noel Bleecker's *Big Music* (Viking).

THE CRAB AND THE CRANE. In: *Jataka Tales,* by E. C. Babbitt. Appleton-Century.

The younger children like all of the Jataka tales: they are simple, dramatic and wise. "Prince Wicked and the Grateful Animals" in the author's *More Jataka Tales* (Appleton-Century) is also fun to tell.

THE DEVIL AND DANIEL WEBSTER, by Stephen Vincent Benét. Rinehart.

One of America's outstanding folk tales told by a poet with zest, humor and beauty of language.

THE FLEA. In: *Picture Tales from Spain,* by Ruth Sawyer. Lippincott.

Storytellers who can sing will find the folk tale collections of Ruth Sawyer useful, since many of their stories contain songs.

EAST O' THE SUN AND WEST O' THE MOON. In: *East o' the Sun and West o' the Moon,* by Gudrun Thorne-Thomsen. Row, Peterson.

These versions of the Asbjornsen and Moe stories, adapted from the Dasent translation by one who is herself a distinguished storyteller, are especially commended to other storytellers.

THE FISHERMAN AND HIS WIFE. In: *Tales from Grimm,* by Wanda Gág. Coward-McCann.

There are many translations of the Grimm Brothers' *Marchen* but Wanda Gág's, in this book and in *More Tales from Grimm* (Coward-McCann), are the best for the storyteller.

THE GOAT WELL. In: *The Fire on the Mountain and Other Ethiopian Stories,* by Harold Courlander and Wolf Leslau. Holt.

The cultures of the East and the West meet in these African folk tales. The two leading figures in this diverting story remind one of Uncle Bouqui and Ti Malice of Haitian folklore fame.

GREEN WILLOW. In: *Green Willow,* by Grace James. Macmillan. o.p.

A haunting story of love and enchantment for older girls. "The Black Bowl" — the Japanese Cinderella story — is equally romantic.

THE HARE AND THE HEDGEHOG. In: *Told Again,* by Walter de la Mare. Knopf.

The English countryside in the Spring provides a sparkling, fresh setting for this old Aesopian fable.

THE HUNGRY OLD WITCH. In: *Tales from Silver Lands,* by Charles J. Finger. Doubleday.

The primitive atmosphere of this Uruguayan Indian story requires an audience of older boys and girls for complete appreciation. It is a good choice for Halloween as is "The Magic Ball."

HOW THE GUBBAUN TRIED HIS HAND AT MATCH-MAKING. In: *The Wonder Smith and His Son,* by Ella Young. Longmans, Green.

The storyteller must tell also "How the Gubbaun Saor Welcomed Home His Daughter" to complete this story of Irish wit and wisdom.

JOHN HENRY AND HIS HAMMER, by Harold Felton. Knopf.

The swing of John Henry's hammer echoes in this rhythmic telling of his mighty deeds.

THE JOLLY TAILOR. In: *The Jolly Tailor and Other Fairy Tales.* Translated from the Polish, by L. M. Borski and K. B. Miller. Longmans, Green.

Mr. Joseph Nitechka mended a tear in the sky and so became king of Pacanów. "King Bartek" is a good choice for the storyhour on Saint Valentine's Day.

KING O'TOOLE AND HIS GOOSE. In: *Celtic Fairy Tales,* by Joseph Jacobs. Putnam. (Dover reprint.)

An hilarious apologue. This book and *More Celtic Fairy Tales* (Putnam) are, like the author's English folk tale collections, invaluable to the storyteller.

THE LAMBIKIN. In: *Indian Fairy Tales,* by Joseph Jacobs. Putnam. (Dover reprint.)

The roots of "The Three Billy Goats Gruff," "The Bun" and "The Three Little Pigs" are in this simple story.

THE LITTLE HUMPBACKED HORSE. In: *Russian Wonder Tales,* by Post Wheeler. Beechhurst Press.

Long romantic tales, these, to spin for an experienced listening audience. *Little Magic Horse* illustrated by Vera Bock (Macmillan) is a metrical version of Peter Ershoff's story.

THE LAST OF THE FROST GIANTS. In: *Canute Whistlewinks,* by Zacharias Topelius. Edited from the translation of C. W. Foss by Frances Jenkins Olcott. Longmans, Green.

A riddle story from Sweden for the Spring storyhour.

THE MAGIC MONKEY, by Plato and Christina Chan. McGraw-Hill. (Whittlesey House).

Monkey is a popular character from Chinese folklore. *The Adventures of Monkey* by Arthur Waley (John Day) tells his story in greater detail.

THE MAIDEN AND THE SARAKIN PUMPKIN. In: *Black Folk Tales,* by Erick Berry. Harper. o.p.

Another good story for Halloween — it is properly scary and ends in a shower of laughter.

THE MATSUYAMA MIRROR. In: *Japanese Fairy Tales,* by Lafcadio Hearn. Liveright.

Filial devotion in this story and connubial difficulties in "Reflections" are the themes of two folk tales about looking-glasses.

MIGHTY MIKKO. In: *Mighty Mikko,* by Parker Fillmore. Harcourt, Brace. o.p.

Humor and marked individuality distinguish this Finnish version of the Puss-in-Boots story.

MR. CROW TAKES A WIFE. In: *Beyond the Clapping Mountains,* by Charles E. Gillham. Macmillan.

These folk tales of the Innuit Indians of Alaska are "a combination of Aesop's fables and Mother Goose rhymes." "Mrs. Longspur's Second Marriage" is also concerned with marital felicity.

A NEW LIST OF STORIES

MR. SAMSON CAT. In: *Picture Tales from the Russian,* by Valery Carrick. Lippincott.

These clear, simply told stories are for the youngest at the storyhour. "Snowflake" is a variant of Miss Shedlock's "Snegourka."

MOLLY WHUPPIE. In: *English Fairy Tales,* by Joseph Jacobs. Putnam. (Dover reprint.)

Every title in this book and its companion volume *More English Fairy Tales* (Putnam) lends itself easily to the art of storytelling.

NUMSKULL AND THE RABBIT. In: *The Panchatantra,* translated by A. W. Ryder. University of Chicago Press.

This story and "How the Rabbit Fooled the Elephant" are so simply told that even the smallest can enjoy their wit and profit by their wisdom.

OLD FIRE DRAGAMAN. In: *The Jack Tales,* by Richard Chase. Houghton Mifflin.

Old World folk tales gathered from storytellers in the Southern Mountains and ready for other tellers of tales to lift from the printed page.

ONE CANDLE POWER. In: *Once the Hodja,* by Alice Geer Kelsey. Longmans, Green.

The Hodja, an urbane character from Turkish folklore, is at times wise, at times foolish, and all these stories about his deeds and misdeeds are good fun to tell.

THE ONE YOU DON'T SEE COMING. In: *The Cow-Tail Switch,* by Harold Courlander and George Herzog. Holt.

A West African folk tale explaining an abstract idea: "The One You Don't See Coming has another name. Some people call him Sleep."

THE PISKEY REVELERS. In: *Piskey Folk,* by Enys Tregarthen. John Day.

A Cornish folk tale of a gay pint neasure and piskeys, party-bent.

THE PRINCESS AND JOSÉ. In: *The Boy Who Could Do Anything,* by Anita Brenner. William R. Scott.

The riddle of the Sphinx is the climax of this Mexican folk tale.

RATA'S SEARCH. In: *The Long Bright Land,* by Edith Howes. Little, Brown. o.p.

Poetical and tellable versions of famous Polynesian legends. "Rata's Search" and "Goblin House" have the quality of hero tales; "Maid of the Mist" and "Hinemoa" are romances for older girls.

SALT. In: *Old Peter's Russian Tales,* by Arthur Ransome. Nelson. (Dover reprint.)

The strength and simplicity of the peasant are in these tales which the author heard when serving as a foreign correspondent in Russia.

SCARFACE. In: *Blackfoot Lodge Tales,* by G. B. Grinnell. Scribner. o.p.

There is dignity and strength in this hero tale of an Indian brave who learned the ritual of the sun.

THE SERPENT OF THE SEA. In: *Zuñi Folk Tales,* by Frank Hamilton Cushing. Knopf. o.p.

A romantic and powerful legend of the Zuñi Pueblo Indians.

THE SHEPHERD'S NOSEGAY. In: *The Shoemaker's Apron,* by Parker Fillmore. Harcourt, Brace.

A merry tale to tell in the Spring. The section in this collection of Czechoslovak folk tales called "Five Nursery Tales" is recommended to the storyteller for use with the younger children.

A NEW LIST OF STORIES

SEVEN SIMEONS: A RUSSIAN TALE, retold and illustrated by Boris Artzybasheff. Viking. o.p.

A robust story that can also be found in *Crimson Fairy Book,* by Andrew Lang. New edition. (Longmans, Green).

THE SHOOTING-MATCH AT NOTTINGHAM TOWN. In: *The Merry Adventures of Robin Hood,* by Howard Pyle. Scribner. (Dover reprint.)

In *Some Merry Adventures of Robin Hood* (Scribner) the Howard Pyle versions of the Sherwood Forest romances have been adapted and simplified. If the storyteller can sing, Anne Malcolmson's *Song of Robin Hood* (Houghton Mifflin) will be useful.

THE SEEPING BEAUTY. In: *All the French Fairy Tales,* by Charles Perrault. Retold by Louis Untermeyer. Didier.

The version given here contains the entire Sleeping Beauty story; the second part is not generally familiar. The illustrations are the classic ones of Gustave Doré.

SOME GOES UP AND SOME GOES DOWN. In: *The Favorite Uncle Remus,* by Joel Chandler Harris. Houghton Mifflin.

A storyteller must have at least a drop of Southern blood in his veins to do justice to these inimitable folk tales.

THE STONE LION. In: *Tales from Timbuktu,* by A. C. Smedley. Harcourt, Brace. o.p.

A Tibetan folk tale, unusual in plot and atmosphere. It can also be found in Mary Gould Davis's *A Baker's Dozen.* (Harcourt, Brace).

THE STONECUTTER. In: *Crimson Fairy Book,* by Andrew Lang. New edition. Longmans, Green. (Dover reprint.)

A Japanese version of the cumulative wishing story which Miss Shedlock calls "Hafiz, the Stone-Cutter."

THE STORY OF URASHIMA TARO, THE FISHER LAD. In: *The Japanese Fairy Book,* by Hei Theodora Ozaki. Dutton. (Dover reprint.)

The oriental Rip Van Winkle story. "Momotaro, or the Story of the Son of a Peach" is the Tom Thumb of Japan.

THE THREE MAGI. In: *The Tiger and the Rabbit,* by Pura Belpré. Houghton Mifflin.

A Puerto Rican story for Twelfth Night that has its roots in Spanish folklore.

THE THREE PRINCESSES IN THE MOUNTAIN SO BLUE. In: *East of the Sun and West of the Moon,* by Ingri and Edgar Parin d'Aulaire. Viking. o.p.

Appropriately enough, the princesses in this Northern folk tale are carried off by a giant snowflake. These retellings from the Dasent translation of Asbjornsen and Moe have been revitalized by the author-artists' Norwegian backgrounds.

TI, TIRITI, TI. In: *Italian Fairy Tales,* by Luigi Capuana. Dutton. o.p.

A Tuscan folk tale told at the time of harvest. The Italian stories in this collection, and those in the author's *Golden Feather* (Dutton), are fresh and new with few variants from the folklore of other countries.

THE TIGER, THE BRAHMAN AND THE JACKAL. In: *Indian Fairy Tales,* by Joseph Jacobs. Putnam. (Dover reprint.)

A classic story in folklore wherein a situation is cleverly re-enacted so that justice may be administered.

THE TSAR SALTAN. In: *Skazki,* by Ida Zeitlin. Rinehart. o.p.

One of Pushkin's *Skazki* retold in distinguished prose and beautifully illustrated. "The Sleeping Tsarevna and the Seven Giants" is a romantic Russian variant of "Snow White and the Seven Dwarfs."

A NEW LIST OF STORIES

THE TWO YOUTHS WHOSE FATHER WAS UNDER THE SEA. In: *The Big Tree of Bunlahy,* by Padraic Colum. Macmillan. o.p.

A mystical Irish witch story.

UNCLE BOUQUI AND TI MALICE GO FISHING. In: *Uncle Bouqui of Haiti,* by Harold Courlander. Morrow.

Two delightful folk tale characters in their roles of fooler and fooled: Ti Malice — crafty, sly, conniving; Uncle Bouqui — kindly, gentle, gullible.

WAKAIMA AND THE CLAY MAN. In: *Wakaima and the Clay Man,* by E. Balintuma Kalibala and Mary Gould Davis. Longmans, Green.

The African source of the Tar Baby story.

WAR BETWEEN THE CROCODILES AND KANTCHIL. In: *Kantchil's Lime Pit and Other Stories from Indonesia,* by Harold Courlander. Harcourt Brace.

All the folk tales in Harold Courlander's collections have been gathered from native sources, consequently the storyteller finds in them not only the wisdom of an oral tradition but the immediacy of a living one.

THE WEE RED MAN. In: *The Donegal Wonder Book,* by Seumas MacManus. Lippincott.

This hearty Irish yarn reels off at a lively rate in support of the briskness of its action.

THE WHITE MUSTANG. In: *Yankee Doodle's Cousins,* by Anna Malcolmson. Houghton Mifflin.

A good collection of American historical-legendary tales. This one explains the origin of painted ponies on the Western plains.

THE WHITE CAT. In: *The White Cat and Other Old French Fairy Tales,* by Mme. Le Comtesse D'Aulnoy. Arranged by Rachel Field and drawn by E. MacKinstry. Macmillan. o.p.

Text, format and illustration mirror perfectly the color and romance of the French court of Louis XIV. Another version of "The White Cat" is in *Blue Fairy Book* by Andrew Lang. 1948 Edition. Longmans, Green.

WHITEBEAR WHITTINGTON. In: *Grandfather Tales,* by Richard Chase. Houghton Mifflin.

"East o' the Sun and West o' the Moon" as told today in the Old English idiom of the Southern Appalachian Mountain people.

WIND AN' WAVE AN' WANDHERIN' FLAME. In: *The Sons o' Cormac,* by Aldis Dunbar. Dutton.

All of the folk tales in this collection are beautifully told, but this one and "Ethlenn o' the Mist" are marked especially by their musical prose and the mood they evoke of a far-off time.

BOOKS FOR THE STORYTELLER

THE ART OF THE STORY-TELLER, by Marie L. Shedlock Dover Publications, Inc.

THE WAY OF THE STORYTELLER, by Ruth Sawyer. Viking.

MYTHOLOGY, by Edith Hamilton. Little, Brown.

Myths of the Greeks, Romans and Norsemen.

GODS AND HEROES. Myths and Epics of Ancient Greece, by Gustav Schwab. Pantheon.

Translated from the German text and its Greek sources by Olga Marx and Ernst Morwitz. Introduction by Werner Jaeger.

A NEW LIST OF STORIES

THE FOLKTALE, by Stith Thompson. Dryden Press.

THE PANCHATANTRA. Translated from the Sanskrit, by Arthur W. Ryder. University of Chicago Press.

ENGLISH FAIRY TALES, collected by Joseph Jacobs. Putnam. (Dover reprint.)

The "Notes and References" are especially recommended to the storyteller.

GRIMM'S FAIRY TALES. Complete edition. Pantheon.

"The text of this edition is based on the translation of Margaret Hunt. Introduction by Padraic Colum. Folkloristic commentary by Joseph Campbell."

TRUE AND UNTRUE AND OTHER NORSE TALES, edited and compiled by Sigrid Undset. Knopf.

Madame Undset's introduction, a brief and scholarly treatise on the folk tale, is salutary reading for all storytellers.

RUSSIAN FAIRY TALES. Pantheon.

Selected from the collection of Aleksandr Afanas'ev. "Translated by Norbert Guterman. Folkloristic commentary by Roman Jakobson."

THE FOUNTAIN OF YOUTH, by Padraic Colum. Macmillan.

Padraic Colum, himself a storyteller, has "reshaped" in this book thirteen of his own tales for other storytellers and written an essay on their mutual art.

BOOKS FOR BOYS AND GIRLS, edited by Lillian H. Smith. Second edition. Toronto Public Library. Ryerson Press.

Three sections of this annotated bibliography — Fairy Tales, Myths, Epic, Saga and Heroic Romance — are especially helpful to the beginning storyteller in building a background.

STORIES TO TELL TO CHILDREN, revised and edited by Laura E. Cathon, Kathryn Kohberger, Virginia A. Russell. Sixth edition. Boys and Girls Department. Carnegie Library of Pittsburgh.

An interesting listing of parallels and variants of folk tales is given in this bibliography.

FOLLOWING THE FOLK TALES AROUND THE WORLD, by Mary Gould Davis. In: *Folklore.* Compton's Pictured Encyclopedia.

One of two articles reprinted from Compton's and issued as a single booklet. The article, with its bibliography, can be found in the Encyclopedia itself under "Storytelling."

STORIES: A List of Stories to Tell and to Read Aloud. Alphabetically arranged, followed by a subject index. Compiled by Eulalie Steinmetz. Fourth edition. The New York Public Library.

NOTE OF ACKNOWLEDGMENT

My thanks are due to: Mrs. Josephine Dodge Daskam Bacon, for permission to use an extract from "The Madness of Philip," and to her publishers, Charles Scribner's Sons.

To Messrs. Houghton Mifflin, for permission to use extract from "Thou Shalt Not Preach," by Mr. John Burroughs.

To Messrs. Macmillan and Co., for permission to use "Milking Time," of Miss Rossetti.

To Mrs. William Sharp, for permission to use passage from "The Divine Adventure," by "Fiona MacLeod.

To Miss Ethel Clifford, for permission to use the poem of "The Child."

To Mr. James Whitcomb Riley and the Bobbs Merrill Co., for permission to use "The Treasure of the Wise Man."

To Professor Ker, for permission to quote from "Sturla the Historian."

To Mr. John Russell, for permission to print in full, "A Saga."

To Messrs. Longmans, Green, and Co., for permission to use "The Two Frogs," from the Violet Fairy Book, and "To Your Good Health," from the Crimson Fairy Book.

To Mr. Heinemann and Lady Glenconner, for permission to reprint "The Water Nixie," by Pamela Tennant, from "The Children and the Pictures."

To Mr. Maurice Baring and the Editor of *The Morning Post,* for permission to reprint "The Blue Rose" from *The Morning Post.*

To Dr. Walter Rouse and Mr. J. M. Dent, for permission to reprint from "The Talking Thrush" the story of "The Wise Old Shepherd."

To Rev. R. L. Gales, for permission to use the article on "Nursery Rhymes" from the *Nation.*

To Mr. Edmund Gosse, for permission to use extracts from "Father and Son."

To Messrs. Chatto & Windus, for permission to use "Essay on Child's Play" (from *Virginibus Puerisque*) and other papers.

To Mr. George Allen & Co., for permission to use "Ballad for a Boy," by W. Cory, from "Ionica."

To Professor Bradley, for permission to quote from his essay on "Poetry and Life."

To Mr. P. A. Barnett, for permission to quote from "The Commonsense of Education."

To Mr. James Stephens, for permission to reprint "The Man and the Boy."

To Mr. Harold Barnes, for permission to use version of "The Proud Cock."

To Mrs. Arnold Glover, for permission to print two of her stories.

To Miss Emilie Poulson, for permission to use her translation of Björnsen's poem.

To George Routledge & Son, for permission to use stories from "Eastern Stories and Fables."

NOTE OF ACKNOWLEDGMENT

To Mrs. W. K. Clifford, for permission to quote from "Very Short Stories."

To Mr. W. Jenkyn Thomas and Mr. Fisher Unwin, for permission to use "Arthur in the Cave" from the Welsh Fairy Book.

To Miss Katherine Wallis, of the London County Council, for valuable additions to chapter of questions.

A CATALOG OF SELECTED

DOVER BOOKS

IN ALL FIELDS OF INTEREST

A CATALOG OF SELECTED DOVER BOOKS IN ALL FIELDS OF INTEREST

THE RIME OF THE ANCIENT MARINER, Gustave Doré, S.T. Coleridge. Doré's finest work, 34 plates capture moods, subtleties of poem. Full text. 77pp. 9¼ × 12. 22305-1 Pa. $4.95

SONGS OF INNOCENCE, William Blake. The first and most popular of Blake's famous "Illuminated Books," in a facsimile edition reproducing all 31 brightly colored plates. Additional printed text of each poem. 64pp. 5¼ × 7. 22764-2 Pa. $3.50

AN INTRODUCTION TO INFORMATION THEORY, J.R. Pierce. Second (1980) edition of most impressive non-technical account available. Encoding, entropy, noisy channel, related areas, etc. 320pp. 5⅜ × 8½. 24061-4 Pa. $4.95

THE DIVINE PROPORTION: A STUDY IN MATHEMATICAL BEAUTY, H.E. Huntley. "Divine proportion" or "golden ratio" in poetry, Pascal's triangle, philosophy, psychology, music, mathematical figures, etc. Excellent bridge between science and art. 58 figures. 185pp. 5⅜ × 8½. 22254-3 Pa. $3.95

THE DOVER NEW YORK WALKING GUIDE: From the Battery to Wall Street, Mary J. Shapiro. Superb inexpensive guide to historic buildings and locales in lower Manhattan: Trinity Church, Bowling Green, more. Complete Text; maps. 36 illustrations. 48pp. 3⅞ × 9¼. 24225-0 Pa. $2.50

NEW YORK THEN AND NOW, Edward B. Watson, Edmund V. Gillon, Jr. 83 important Manhattan sites: on facing pages early photographs (1875-1925) and 1976 photos by Gillon. 172 illustrations. 171pp. 9¼ × 10. 23361-8 Pa. $7.95

HISTORIC COSTUME IN PICTURES, Braun & Schneider. Over 1450 costumed figures from dawn of civilization to end of 19th century. English captions. 125 plates. 256pp. 8⅜ × 11¼. 23150-X Pa. $7.50

VICTORIAN AND EDWARDIAN FASHION: A Photographic Survey, Alison Gernsheim. First fashion history completely illustrated by contemporary photographs. Full text plus 235 photos, 1840-1914, in which many celebrities appear. 240pp. 6½ × 9¼. 24205-6 Pa. $6.00

CHARTED CHRISTMAS DESIGNS FOR COUNTED CROSS-STITCH AND OTHER NEEDLECRAFTS, Lindberg Press. Charted designs for 45 beautiful needlecraft projects with many yuletide and wintertime motifs. 48pp. 8¼ × 11. 24356-7 Pa. $2.50

101 FOLK DESIGNS FOR COUNTED CROSS-STITCH AND OTHER NEEDLE-CRAFTS, Carter Houck. 101 authentic charted folk designs in a wide array of lovely representations with many suggestions for effective use. 48pp. 8¼ × 11. 24369-9 Pa. $2.25

FIVE ACRES AND INDEPENDENCE, Maurice G. Kains. Great back-to-the-land classic explains basics of self-sufficient farming. The one book to get. 95 illustrations. 397pp. 5⅜ × 8½. 20974-1 Pa. $4.95

A MODERN HERBAL, Margaret Grieve. Much the fullest, most exact, most useful compilation of herbal material. Gigantic alphabetical encyclopedia, from aconite to zedoary, gives botanical information, medical properties, folklore, economic uses, and much else. Indispensable to serious reader. 161 illustrations. 888pp. 6½ × 9¼. (Available in U.S. only) 22798-7, 22799-5 Pa., Two-vol. set $16.45